Assaulted Souls III

by

I0552255

William Blackwell

ASSAULTED SOULS III

Cover Designed by Telemachus Press, LLC

Published by Telemachus Press, LLC

ISBN: 978-1-7389714-9-7 (paperback)

Version 2016.12.16

Acknowledgements

Heartfelt thanks to my loyal and supportive readers, friends and family, the hardworking staff at Telemachus Press, and my editor. Special thanks to the Government of Prince Edward Island for its financial support.

If you prick us do we not bleed? If you tickle us do we not laugh? If you poison us do we not die? And if you wrong us shall we not revenge?

–William Shakespeare

Assaulted Souls III

Chapter One

"We've got incoming," Nathan shouted.

"The only thing incoming is your head," Ed said.

"What's that supposed to mean?" Nathan said.

"Your head ... it's coming in from the cold."

That much was true, Nathan thought. They had been foraging for food earlier on the decimated landscape and the cold wind had chilled him to the bone. But hadn't he killed a rabbit with a crossbow, something he had been unable to do previously? He thought so, but as he closed the metal door to the network of caves and followed Edward Sole, his protector all along, he now realized, his hands were empty. No crossbow. No dead rabbit. Maybe Ed had it? "Do you have the rabbit?"

"What fuckin' rabbit?"

"The one I killed earlier."

"You didn't kill shit."

"I did. I killed a rabbit."

"Like fuck you did."

They walked down a winding dark tunnel, guided by Ed's small flashlight. The beam was so small that Nathan had trouble seeing where he was going. He tripped over a rock, landing hard on his knees.

Ed stopped and trained the small beam on bloody, bare knees. "Watch where you're going—some gnarly rocks in here."

"Tell me about it," Nathan said, wiping away rivulets of blood snaking down his shins. "Fuck sakes."

"Come on," Ed said, turning and continuing on. "We need to get a fire going before it gets too cold."

Shivering, Nathan followed. For the first time he wondered what in the hell he was doing in this freezing wasteland walking around barefoot and bare-chested, with only a pair of torn Levi shorts for protection. And then it hit him like a derailed locomotive travelling at 190 kilometers an hour. He shouldn't be here. No. Not at all. He should be dead. Maybe he was. Escaping District 101 with Doctor Stan Imes and Velvet Jones in a small black submarine, they had been blown to smithereens by an underwater missile. All they wanted was freedom from a government bent on genetic modification, turning them into perfect warriors—warriors who would go to battle at the sound of a simple letter-number combination, or violence-activation code. An enhanced population. Good when you want them to be. Bad when you want them to be. The perfect utopia.

But it hadn't worked out that way at all. More like a dystopia; a place of terror, oppression and deprivation.

Nathan stopped abruptly. "Ed, am I dead?"

"We're all fuckin' dead. You call this living? Fighting savage Neanderthals, mutant animals, fuckin' zombies, and now the Canadian military. What kind of life is it anyway?"

"No ... me. I mean me. Am I dead?"

Ed stopped, turned around and shone the flashlight in Nathan's eyes. "Not that I can tell. You look very much alive to me."

"You mean I never left here?"

"We've just been hunting. We left."

"I don't mean that. I mean the Island. I've never left Prince Edward Island? I've never been to District 101, where I was ... enhanced? Where they turned on Doctor Imes because he wasn't getting the desired results with P-744? Where everyone seemed to have their own fuckin' agenda to control the world?"

"I have no clue what you're talking about," Ed said. "I think you've gone bat-shit crazy."

Cold terror gripped Nathan. "No ... no ... no ... it can't be! It can't be! I was on District 101 with Velvet, Melvin Tierney, Captain Sterling, Commander Randall Stiessman ... you see, I know all the names. How could I make them up?"

Ed ignored him.

They arrived at an opening with a vast rocky ceiling and a small rock-lined fire pit in the center. "You've got a vivid imagination," Ed said, approaching the fire pit and sitting down cross-legged. He snapped small branches and threw them into the makeshift pit. "You used to work as a journalist. Journalism is art, I think."

Soon Ed had a respectable blaze going. He warmed his hands on the fire while Nathan just stared around the cave, incredulous, without saying a word. *I've never left here. The accident when the world was normal, before the nuclear bomb was dropped, falling off the roof, the amnesia, maybe it also caused me to go bat-shit crazy, as Ed says. No. That was too real. It has to be real.* And then he did remember. They had escaped Prince Edward Island prior to landing on District 101. Ed had died a hero aiding their escape.

"Ed," Nathan said, "you're dead."

Ed looked at Nathan and grinned. Macabre black war paint lines extended from the corners of his mouth, across his cheeks and along his nose. The shit-eating grin made him look like a demented clown. His beady eyes glowed black and red. "I'm not dead. You can't die. You just pass over to another realm, sometimes worse, sometimes better. Don't worry. Reality and dreams are one and the same, life and death, one and the same. You'd do well to remember that."

A loud boom suddenly rocked the cave. Nathan staggered back, almost falling. The ceiling began cracking and rocks large and small began crashing to the ground. Nathan dove near a cave wall for protection. Ed grinned maniacally, warmed his hands by the fire, and watched. "What are you afraid of? I told you. We can't die."

Water poured through the cracks. The larger network of caves began collapsing.

Ed's face was enveloped by the fire. He grinned knowingly as water poured in and Nathan clung to the jagged edge of a boulder for survival. *But I'm dead.*

The cascading water had no effect on the fire. Instead, it grew, Ed's face growing with it, rising above the pooling water, fiery spears spanning out like a star in motion. "You can't die," Ed said. "Don't worry. I'll meet you in the Second Realm."

Then a massive torrent of rushing water tore through the cave, dislodging Nathan's precarious grip and washing him rapidly down one of many tunnels. He fought to try and keep his head afloat, but the water was too powerful, its volume too great to defeat. His head submerged. He held his breath and counted in his mind. Why? He didn't know, but that was all he could think to do … *one, two, three, four, five …*

When he reached forty-seven he felt his lungs tighten up and begin to ache. He couldn't hold his breath anymore, probably the result of smoking too much for too many years, he thought grimly. He frantically pushed his head to the surface and exhaled. As he inhaled, a wave clapped his face hard and a few mouthfuls of water filled his mouth, pouring into his lungs. He started coughing violently but was instantly submerged by the ferocious flow. He fought to bring his head above water again and finally managed, spewing mouthfuls of water only to inhale and swallow three more mouthfuls, before being swept underwater again.

He repeated the death-defying procedure once more, was swept under water again after inhaling more water and decided it. *Maybe Ed's right. I can't die. Let's hope he's right.*

He opened his mouth and exhaled. Water flowed out. He inhaled. Water flowed in, filling his lungs. He felt the life slowly drain from his body. He closed his eyes, welcoming the blackness, wanting to end it all; end the misery of life in the real world. Maybe life in the Second Realm was much better anyway.

His body felt weightless, like he was floating, somewhere far beyond Earth's gravitational pull. Blackness was replaced by a purple rainbow that slowly transformed into vibrant reds, oranges, greens, blues, yellows—he could even see bright pink at the end of the rainbow. But then the rainbow faded and vanished. It was replaced by something else. A blinding and all-encompassing yellow light, powerful, heat-producing and healing, like the sun's rays.

He smiled serenely. *It's true. The only difference is it's not a white light. It's yellow.* He felt calm, finally at peace. Then a vivid collage of images flashed through his mind and he was overcome by emotion. His life's memorable events, rolling by his mind's eye like a three-dimensional color film on fast-forward. At the good deeds, he smiled, while the bad deeds, indiscretions, and there had been many, produced frowns, the footage of Nathan cheating on his late girlfriend Cadence Whittaker even causing his eyes to well up with tears.

"Cadence," he said. "My true love. I'm coming, baby. I'm coming to be with you forever."

But if this was purgatory, he thought, that halfway judging ground between heaven and hell, would he make it to heaven, had he done enough charitable and selfless deeds to ascend to that hallowed ground?

He didn't know. The intense heat from the blinding light was all at once too much. He shut his eyes and prayed. *God, if you're out there, please, please bring me to heaven to meet Cadence. I need to be with her. Please, please, please …*

******

Nathan felt hot, full lips touch his. The blinding yellow light slowly faded to black. The lips breathed warm breaths into his lungs; *one … count them … two, three, four, five …*

Nathan jerked up, puking yellowish-white foam along with a stream of water, and opened his eyes. When he finished vomiting and coughing, he looked up. Beneath a black and fiery orange turbid sky, penetrating green eyes stared down intently at him. Her lips were pursed. He coughed, puked again and breathed in panicked gasps as a hand gently lifted his head, tilting him to one side. When his head cleared somewhat, he regarded the woman staring at him concernedly

Her, Nathan thought. *It's really her.*

"Cadence," he said weakly, unable to lift his head. "It's really you. God's answered my prayer."

"It's me," Velvet said. "Not Cadence. She's dead. Remember? And, as far as I know, there is no fuckin' God. If there was—" she waved a hand to a rubble-strewn wasteland—"he wouldn't have allowed this shit to happen."

"You ... you saved my life."

"You can thank me later," Velvet said, adjusting the gauze wrapped around her head. It was blotted with blood. "We need to go. They'll be choppers, fighter jets, whatever, coming soon."

"I saw ... I saw the light. We don't really die. Just pass over to another realm. The Second Realm, heaven."

"Tell me about it later," Velvet said, helping Nathan to his feet. "We need to go. Now!"

Doctor Stan Imes stepped forward, grabbing Nathan's other arm, and the three slowly walked, stepping over rubble and bomb-demolished buildings. There were other abandoned-looking turn-of-the-century houses with windows smashed out. The wind whipped up, and a bank of black clouds rolled in, obliterating what little remained of the setting sun.

"Where to?" Velvet asked Imes.

Imes scratched his chin stubble, glancing around. "I think we're in Georgetown, or what's left of it. We need to get to Montague."

They froze, listening to the sound of helicopter rotors in the distance, growing louder. "We've got incoming," Nathan shouted.

Velvet pointed to a two-story brick house with windows intact. "Over there. It's the best of the bunch."

"You've gotta run," Velvet said to Nathan.

"You've got to," Imes said, nudging him.

"I feel weak," Nathan said.

"You should," Velvet said. "You've been dead for over five minutes."

"Push yourself," Imes said. "The adrenaline will take over."

Nathan grunted and groaned, commanding his legs to move faster. They were slow to react, but finally, with the help and prodding of Velvet and Imes, he managed to find a pace akin to a marathon walk. They arrived at the house. Velvet entered the unlocked front door first, and Nathan and Imes stepped in just as the chopper arrived directly overhead.

"We need to get in the basement," Velvet said, extracting a handgun and checking rooms as she walked down a narrow hallway.

Nathan checked his holster, found the handgun intact. He followed Velvet.

She went into the kitchen and noticed a rectangular hump in the throw rug on the floor. She pulled the carpet aside and heaved on a trap door. A loud explosion rocked the front porch. A ball of flame engulfed it and the door blew off its hinges, crashing and splintering on the hallway floor. The blast sent Nathan flying into a countertop. Imes bounced into a kitchen table and fell on his ass.

Velvet clung to the trap door. She lifted it up. "Get in. Quick."

Imes produced a flashlight and led the way. Nathan followed and Velvet closed the trap door just as another bomb smashed through the roof, shaking them while they descended the ladder.

They reached a dirt floor and Imes, looking for an escape route, began shining the flashlight beam as deafening explosions rocked the foundation. He trained it on a small hole in a dirt wall as ceiling boards cracked, splintered and fell. A rat poked its head out, eyeballed them calmly with glowing red eyes, and then skittered away. "In here," Imes said. "It's a tunnel."

Velvet and Nathan crawled in and Imes followed. They crawled down the dark, dank-smelling tunnel. It wound down for about fifty feet before leveling out. Every so often, bomb blasts would shake the ground and shower them with dirt.

But after a few minutes of crawling, the bomb blasts grew faint, the ground beneath their hands and knees becoming firm and steady.

They stopped, all breathing deeply.

Between gasps, Nathan said, "That house is toast."

"Keep going," Velvet said. "This tunnel could cave at any time."

They carried on.

Eventually the dirt tunnel led to a straight steel tunnel. They stopped as Imes shone the beam down what was obviously a sewer main. The beam illuminated little red dots, hundreds of beady eyes, surrounded by blackness, staring at them. The rats squeaked and squirmed, slowly and methodically scattering farther into the steel tubular abyss.

Very faintly, chopper rotors thumped outside.

A loud explosion shook the ground and a wall of dirt caved in about twenty feet behind them.

"One way out," Velvet said, glancing back as Imes trained the beam on the mound of rock and dirt that had collapsed.

"We hope it leads out," Nathan said.

"Shut up and listen," Velvet said.

They obliged. The faint sound of chopper rotors was coming from wherever the sewer main led to.

"You're right," Nathan said. "There must be an opening there."

"Got to be," Imes agreed. "The rats went that way."

They moved along for fifteen minutes amidst squeaking and scurrying rats and arrived at a partially dislodged manhole cover. "There," Imes said, pointing to it. "Let's get out of here."

They climbed up a steel ladder. Nathan poked his head up just in time to see the black shadow of a man point a rocket launcher at a descending chopper, fire, and blow it into a raining shower of debris and flames. The shadowy figure disappeared behind a dilapidated house.

"We've got company," Nathan said, climbing out onto cracked pavement and extending a hand to Velvet. She took it, pulled herself up onto the road and stood up, Imes following. "Someone blew up the chopper."

"It's The Neanderthals, likely," Imes said, pointing a tiny beam of light onto a nearby house window. A shadowy black arm extended briefly from the house and then vanished instantly.

"Come on," Velvet said. "We're in no position to find out."

The wind whipped mini debris-tornadoes through dimly lit, desolate streets as they searched for a safe place to hole up for the night. But no chopper rotors could be heard. At least for the time being, the military had called off its search-and-destroy mission.

"Over there," Velvet said, pointing to a brick house that sat beside two demolished remnants of what had once been homes on a quiet and peaceful residential street in a quaint historic town on a calm, beautiful, Gentle Island. "There's a light on."

Behind sheer bay-window blinds, candlelight flickered in the living room.

They walked up the concrete path leading to a small porch. Velvet knocked three times on the front door and they waited in silence. A metallic click echoed from inside the house—the hammer of a gun cocking.

"Get down," Velvet yelled, pushing Nathan away and diving onto the small porch.

They ducked.

A loud shotgun blast rang out and buckshot tore through the front door, sending splintering wood and glass flying everywhere.

Then the weak but determined voice of an old woman: "Get the fuck outta here ... I said get the fuck outta here if you know what's good for ya."

The door creaked open, its deadbolt lock destroyed by the blast.

"We mean you no harm," Velvet shouted. "We're in trouble. We need help."

The shotgun fired again and more buckshot splintered glass and wood, raining down a shower of debris onto three prostrate bodies on a porch.

The blast reverberated into the night eerily, caught a gust of wind, and was swept away.

"Poke yer head out," the woman said, her voice growing weaker. "I dare ya."

"We're not Neanderthals," Velvet offered. "We mean to kill them."

They heard a clang inside, like the noise a shotgun would make dropping to a wooden floor.

"Wait here," Velvet said, getting up, kicking out what remained of the door and stepping into the house, gun drawn.

She saw an old white-haired waif of a woman sitting on a tattered armchair, blood oozing from a gunshot wound to her right shoulder, a hand clenched tightly on a hand grenade, another hand hovering shakily over the metal pin. "Take one step closer and get blown to bits," the woman said.

Velvet kept her weapon trained on the woman's wrinkled and grimacing face. To say she looked like death warmed over would have been an understatement. Velvet froze in the hallway. "You're injured," she said.

Nathan stood up, drew his gun and stepped inside.

Imes stood up, peered into the hallway, but stayed outside.

"I said stop," the woman demanded, clenching the pin.

Nathan stopped. "Let us help you," he said. "There's a doctor in the house."

There was a moment of tense silence and the woman finally removed her hand from the pin. "You're not Neanderthals?" she asked.

"No," Nathan and Velvet said.

"Who are you then?"

"We're survivors ... just trying to stay alive," Velvet said. "Let us help you."

"Where you from?" the woman asked, forefinger crawling closer to the pin.

"We're from here," Velvet said. "We were on District 101, the government's experimental island, before it was destroyed by a tsunami wave."

"I heard about that place," the woman said. "Nothing good."

"No," Velvet said.

"All right," the woman said. "Help me or kill me. My time has about come anyway. An end would be good."

"There's no end," Nathan said. "You pass over to the Second Realm."

"He a bible thumper?" the woman asked, relaxing her skinny arms. The grenade popped out of her hand and rolled down her knee.

Velvet dove, extending a hand and catching it just a few inches before it hit the wooden floor.

"I see you've learned a few things about survival," the woman said as Velvet stared up at her, holding the grenade with an unsteady hand.

Velvet nodded and slowly stood up.

"I'm Mary Anne," the woman said. "Mary Anne Sole."

******

Twenty minutes later, Doctor Imes had removed the bullet from Mary Anne's shoulder, poured alcohol over the wound—a full bottle of vodka was all he could find—and cauterized it with a butter knife he had heated bright orange on a small propane torch he had found in a spare upper bedroom, alongside an arsenal of weapons. During the procedure, Mary Anne had taken three large swallows of the vodka. She winced when the bullet was extracted and the wound cauterized, but didn't utter a single cry of pain. She was a trooper.

Nathan found a few chunks of plywood and bits of door casing, and nailed them to the front door while Velvet rummaged around in the kitchen, found three tins of canned tuna, a can opener, three forks and a serving tray. She brought them into the living room, setting the tray on a coffee table beside a flickering candle.

They ate tuna while Mary Anne pulled on the vodka. "I don't want to ruin my alcohol buzz," she replid when Velvet had asked if she was hungry. "But help yourselves."

While they ate, Nathan studied Mary Anne. Something she'd said, and her hollow unfocused eyes, reminded him of someone. Then it came to him. "Did you say you're Mary Anne Sole?"

Through vacant eyes glittering orange from the candle's reflection, she nodded.

"Do you know Edward Sole?" Nathan asked.

"My grandson," Mary Anne said. "He was killed by The Neanderthals."

"He saved our lives," Nathan said, pointing to Velvet. "He died a hero. But he's in the Second Realm now, and happy I think."

Mary Anne swallowed more vodka, cradling the bottle in her lap when she finished. "Such a lost soul Ed was. But a heart of gold once you got to know him."

"He was my neighbor and friend," Nathan said. "I believe he's still looking out for us. For you too, probably."

Mary Anne arched an eyebrow. "Ed had a hard enough time looking out for himself, never mind anyone else."

"That was then," Nathan said. "This is now. I died escaping District 101. Velvet here brought me back to life. She died escaping 101. Imes brought her back to life." He turned to Velvet. "Did you see the other side, when you were dead?"

"I didn't see fuck all," Velvet said.

"I saw the other side," Nathan said. "I was there with your grandson. He told me to embrace death as merely part of the journey, part of the passage into the Second Realm."

"It all sounds rather touching," Mary Anne said. Her pink nightgown had slid part way down her arm and she pulled it up so it concealed the white gauze wrapped around the injured shoulder. "But I don't believe in any of that. To me, when we're gone, that's it—a big, black, meaningless, lifeless void is all that remains. Do you know I've lost a husband, three kids, three dogs, two cats, two sisters and six grandsons, Ed among them? I haven't seen any visions showing a better place than here. Mind you, it wouldn't take much to beat this place, would it? Even hell, I'm sure, would be better than this. I've outlived my entire family. Do you know how hard it is for a mother to outlive her children?"

Her voice trailed off. Her eyes moistened and a lone tear slipped down her cheek. She ignored it, her gaze settling on the vodka bottle that had been three-quarters full not a half-hour ago. She raised it, contemplating another drink, and then set it down in her lap. "I should offer you a drink," she said. "There's wine under the kitchen sink. Join the party."

Velvet stood. "Don't mind if I do." She raised her eyebrows at Imes and Nathan.

"Sure," Imes said. "I'll take a nightcap before I turn in. Awfully tired."

Nathan raised a thumb. "Sure."

"Let's have a right PEI-style shindig," Mary Anne said, lifting the bottle with renewed vigor and swallowing two mouthfuls before setting it between her legs.

By the time Velvet returned with the drinks, Mary Anne was snoring lightly. Her grip on the vodka bottle had loosened. She clung to it with three fingers.

Nathan slid it from her grasp and put it on the coffee table. Then he lifted his glass of wine and raised it to Velvet and Doctor Imes. "To making it this far. And a special toast to Velvet for saving my life."

Chapter Two

After his visit with Ed in the afterlife, or Second Realm as Ed preferred to call it, Nathan wasn't sure how much value to place on his life, or life in general for that matter. Wasn't the Second Realm a much better place than the day-to-day torture of his current existence? It was a rhetorical question, he thought, as he curled up in a sleeping bag on a single bed in a guest bedroom of Mary Anne's house and tried unsuccessfully to turn off his mind and get some shut-eye.

Three glasses of wine later, he and Velvet had carried a passed-out Mary Anne to bed, discussed tomorrow's agenda—somehow get to Doctor Imes's underground laboratory in Montague—and Velvet had recapped for Nathan's benefit what exactly happened after they had escaped the ferocious tsunami wave that had destroyed District 101. Using the submarine's sophisticated radar systems, Imes had fortunately been able to detect the incoming underwater missile. Close to the shores of PEI at the time, they had donned life jackets. Imes proceeded with a rapid ascent of the vessel. But fifty feet from the surface, he realized they weren't going to make it in time. So they had climbed into an eject chamber and were fired like human torpedoes into the ocean toward the surface. It was then the missile struck the submarine and a massive underwater explosion sent them rocketing in different directions. Nathan's life jacket had slipped off in the blast. He had inhaled water and died. As he slowly drifted to the ocean depths, it was Velvet who spotted him, recovered his body, swam to the shores of Georgetown with it, and revived him.

Recalling the story, Nathan almost wished he had met a permanent watery grave rather than the five or so minutes he had stopped breathing. Even though he and Ed had had their differences in the past, he figured life with Ed—and Cadence—would be much better than the hell here.

And there was something about the way in which Mary Anne—Ed's grandmother, what were the chances of meeting her in this hellhole?—had looked at him when he mentioned the Second Realm. While Mary Anne dismissed the idea of a heaven or hell, her eyes said something else; that she had been to hell and back, maybe to heaven and back, but was unwilling to acknowledge or discuss it.

But Nathan now had a strong desire to go the Second Realm, rid himself of all the haunting nightmares, an engineered physicality and personality that could turn violent and deadly in a heartbeat. Leave forever the new world order where the government and other savage mutants operated with self-serving agendas, where humans were as expendable as disposable lighters.

A special toast to Velvet for saving my life. Did I mean it? No. The Second Realm. A fresh start. Not a death wish at all. A wish for a better life.

He tossed and turned on the small bed, trying to push the suicidal thoughts away; hoping against all hope that he could find some meaning in this wasteland, find some reason to learn to appreciate life again.

But, after fifteen minutes of grasping for some glass-half-full image to cling to, what assaulted Nathan's soul were the words Ed had uttered nonchalantly in the afterlife: "*You can't die. You just pass over to another realm, sometimes worse, sometimes better. Don't worry. Reality and dreams are one and the same, life and death, one and the same. You'd do well to remember that."*

Nathan sat bolt upright, forgetting about sleep. It wasn't coming easy anyway. He stared around the room at the floral-patterned wallpaper, black demon-like shadows shrinking and growing, shrinking and growing, as a bedside table candle flickered, blown by intermittent wind gusts from a partially open window. He got out of bed, closed the window, and stared out at the blackness. There were no stars in the sky—probably obscured by cloud cover, he thought—and no moon. Only a few small yellow and orange dots—flickering flames scattered across a black and bleak landscape; probably others, struggling to survive, or perhaps they were debris fires, the remnants of recent attacks.

He didn't know why, but looking at the little orange dots brought back horrible memories of trying to survive; experiences he knew had left permanent scars. Attacks from mutant seagulls, zombies, watching frothing mutant pigs rampaging through the streets, and the most horrible of all, the attacks from the savage and opportunistic Neanderthals. *They* had raped and killed Cadence, *they* had nearly killed him, *they* were responsible for Nathan fleeing the Island, only to end up in the clutches of a government bent on bending his will. And the questions that he had forgotten, or he had managed to block from his mind, suddenly bombarded his senses.

Who dropped the bombs that devastated most of Canada, most of the world? The North Koreans, according to Commander Stiessman. Nathan doubted it. Who was responsible for the follow-up bio-chemical attack? The North

Koreans, like he had been told? He doubted that, too. And what about the military? They were still out there, to be sure. The ever-present bell tolling in his eardrums—shell-shock from the recent traumatic tunnel bombing—was all the proof he needed of that. Why did the Canadian and American military still want him dead? *It's obvious, bonehead. A cover-up. Yeah, but how much can they cover up?*

If that wasn't enough, maybe the zombies were also on PEI, although he had heard they only populated Newfoundland. But who knew if they could develop the wherewithal to man boats and get to PEI. *Do they eat flesh? Don't they all? They're zombies, bonehead. What do you think zombies do?*

As the bell tolls. As the church bell tolls. As the bell in your fuckin' head tolls, you go nuts. Stop it, stop it, stop all the thoughts. You have one moment. It's now. Live for it. And hope that Ed was right. That there is a better place, where you can be with Cadence.

Feeling more alone than he had ever felt, Nathan realized with grim, terrible certainty and hopelessness his life would never, ever be the same again. He suddenly wanted more than ever to talk to someone, have some company to calm his troubled mind, a mind he felt was on the precipice of insanity.

He revisited the horror movie he had watched while dead, the fast-forwarded dramatic film clicking through his mind's eye, poignantly capturing his life's journey in all its glory, in all its gory detail. One by one the images shuffled past, pulling him into madness.

He shuddered, retreating from the window, rubbing the goose bumps on his arms. He returned to the bed and sat down. But the thoughts of Cadence led to thoughts of Velvet and, watching the tent growing in his jeans, he realized he wanted something with her again that he had so enjoyed in the past. Was it the P-744 fucking him up? He didn't know, but as he left the bedroom, closing the slowly creaking door behind, he hoped Velvet was feeling the same way; that she too right this very minute was being sent to insatiable levels of arousal by the yet unresolved side effects of P-744. *Who knows, maybe Imes can fix us up if we get to his lab? Do I want him to fix us up? Maybe I'm growing to like this feeling. Just talk to her. Talk to her, talk to her, talk to her—fuck her—no, no, no, no, talk only, talk only. Fuck only. Fuck you, talk only you fuckhead. Talk, talk, talk and more fucking talk. Blah, blah, blah. That's all I need.*

It took Nathan a few seconds to realize he was standing outside Velvet's door, looking at but not seeing the antique decorative glass door handle. He wondered how long he had been there, how long his mind had gapped out. He knocked on the door. He wasn't here to try and solve his fucked up enhancements. He heard a stirring behind the door, the shifting of a body, the squeaking of bed springs.

"Velvet," Nathan whispered. "Velvet, it's me. I need to talk." *You need to fuck.* "Let me in. Please. I'm going fucking crazy."

"It's open," Velvet said. "Come in."

Nathan went it. He wasn't expecting such an erotic spectacle, and his eyes and something else bulged at the sight of it. Velvet lay on her back on the double bed, a blanket pulled down to her waist, exposing her naked and perky breasts. The bedside candle gave them a warm, seductive glow. One hand was outside the blanket massaging an erect nipple while the other was underneath it. The bobbing motion of the blanket—up and down, up and down—told Nathan exactly what she was doing. Masturbating. Her eyes were partially closed, her lips pursed up in intense satisfaction.

"Wow," Nathan said, moving toward the bed. "You too?"

"I'm so horny I could fuck a bedpost," Velvet said without interrupting her smooth stroke.

"No need. I'm here."

"Come inside me," she said with a soft moan. "Right fucking now."

"I need to fuck you," Nathan said, undressing.

Velvet tossed the blanket aside, exposing her beautiful nakedness. She removed her middle finger from its orifice, licked it deliciously, and opened her arms to Nathan, who had already stripped down to the buff. "You do," she said, panting with pleasure. "You do indeed."

Chapter Three

"You go if I say you do," Mason Mulligan said, slamming a fist down hard on a pock-marked coffee table. Beer cans and cigarette-butt stuffed ashtrays flew, beers foaming and emptying, rolling off the unbalanced table. Mason steadied the coffee table with one hand, saving his rolling, frothing beer with the other. He put the foaming can to his acne-scarred, pudgy face and, not wanting to waste a drop, drank from the fountain of broken dreams.

Joey Zidewick wasn't so lucky. His beer can had bounced and rolled onto his lap, and was draining onto his crotch before he realized what had happened. He picked up the empty can lodged between his legs, frowned, and dropped it on the cave floor. It made a tinny sound as it rolled a few feet and stopped.

Seven other Neanderthal members sat on battered couches in the network of caves, some playing cards by candlelight and gas lantern, others drinking and chatting. They grew silent, craned necks, watched and waited. They were waiting to see if Joey, Mason's whipping boy, would finally grow some stones and stand up to the ruthless Neanderthal leader.

Earlier, while out on a scavenging mission around the network of caves located near Murray River, perhaps thirty minutes by vehicle from Georgetown where Nathan and Velvet were engaged in carnal extra-curricular activities, The Neanderthals had watched with interest as military choppers bombed Georgetown buildings. Looking through a high-powered telescope, Mason couldn't see the choppers. The sky was black and overcast, the choppers too far. But he did see the huge fireball explosions resulting from missile strikes. And he wondered what new target, or targets, the military had set its sights on now. And why?

So, an hour or so later, after a meal of canned beans and canned beer, Mason had ordered Joey to take one of the beat-up pick-up trucks the Neanderthals had in its fleet, pick another volunteer from the other card-carrying—at least card-playing—members, and go investigate.

But Joey had uncharacteristically responded like a rebellious, petulant teenager, telling his boss, "I don't want to go. I'm too tired."

That response had infuriated Mason, who before the apocalypse was doing life without the possibility of parole for raping and murdering sixteen teenage girls. But the end of one world—the beginning of a new world order—had given Mason (his cell-mates, some now Neanderthals, respectfully referred to him as Mason Danger) a new lease on life, a life where he could rule by fear and intimidation. After law and order had collapsed, chaos born of the fundamental need to survive had erupted, and prison guards abandoned their posts, escape from the maximum security facility in neighboring New Brunswick had been as easy as strolling out of a supermarket. Of course Mason had made the best of it, not least of all because it's what his late criminal-minded older brother Karl Mulligan would have wanted for his younger sibling. To make the highest and best use of your time, be goal-oriented, get things done. Don't ever let others stand in the way of your goals, however malicious and ill-intentioned they might be. "Make a plan and stick to the fuckin' plan," as Karl used to say.

Recollecting the axiom that had propelled him to the top of the savages, Mason scratched the stubble on his chin, brushed his mop of black hair away from beady eyes glowing red from the candle's reflection, wrinkled his brow and addressed Joey, who was staring again at what looked like a piss stain on his crotch. Mason detested having to give orders more than once, almost as much as he detested the geeky-looking dork sitting in front of him. Truth be told, it was more of a love-hate relationship. In the joint, Joey had been the unwilling recipient of some less than consensual anal intercourse at the big man's aggressive hands and equally aggressive member.

"Did you hear what I said, you skinny little fuck?" Mason asked, clenching his right fist as he glared at Joey.

Joey adjusted his tattered blue Kokanee baseball cap sideways—he always did that when he was nervous—and, like a scorned puppy dog, slowly lifted sad brown eyes to the boss. Then he stood up, wiped cigarette ashes and beer foam off his jeans, and said, "I heard you, boss. I'm sorry." He looked over at the group of seven, a few grinning. Not many of them liked Joey, a rather timid misfit. "I'll go now. I'll take Brut, if that's okay?"

"I don't care who the fuck you take," Mason snapped, whipping an empty beer can at Joey, who ducked a little too late as it struck him on the side of the forehead. It dented, echoed hollowly, then clinked and clanked across the uneven ground. "I said pick a fuckin' volunteer. I didn't tell you who to pick. I don't care who the fuck you pick ... just pick someone and get the hell out of here. Now!"

Joey stepped toward a black hole, the round entrance to a tunnel that led outside. He stopped and glanced at Brut (Bruce

Gangston was his real name), a hulk of a man, and one of the bigger and brawnier Neanderthals. "You coming?"

Brut stood, belched loudly, flicked a cigarette butt on the ground, and winked. "I'll hold yer hand," he said in a booming baritone voice.

Joey reached the black hole. He picked up an AK-47 leaning against a rock wall, slung it over his shoulder, and waited for Brut.

Brut arrived, slung an AK-47 over his shoulder along with two bullet belts, and checked his two side holsters. Satisfied they contained loaded handguns, he stepped into the black hole and Joey followed.

"Hold up," Mason shouted.

Brut kept going.

Joey turned around and peered out of the darkness. "Yes, boss?"

"You see anyone new in Georgetown, bring them back alive. I want to find out why the fuckin' military is creeping around here again. You got that?"

"Will do, boss." Joey turned and began leaving.

"You fuckin' better," Mason said. "Cause the next thing I throw at your hollow head won't be an empty beer can."

He stood up, flashing angry eyes at the men, who had resumed their card game and were talking in hushed tones. "I think I'm gonna catch me a bit o' shut-eye," Mason said. "So keep it down."

The men nodded, almost in unison.

Mason walked toward another black hole, stopped abruptly, and scratched his beer belly, which poked out from beneath an ill-fitting, dirt-stained white t-shirt. There's always

Leanne, Mason thought. Leanne was a middle-aged woman who the Neanderthals had captured three days ago. They had found her holed up in a root cellar in a partially demolished two-story house on a nearby rural acreage. Looking gaunt, malnourished and fearful, Leanne was chewing on a dead rat when Mason kicked away the wooden planks concealing the root cellar and found her. The discovery led to her kidnapping, what Mason liked to call "mild torture" and repeated rape. Along with Mason, the other savages, excepting only Joey and Brut, had also participated. *One good stab, a good fucking, before I turn in should just about fix me up for the night.* Mason belched loudly and asked: "Is that scrawny bitch still in the black hole?" That's how Mason referred to the smallest cave dwelling in the network of caves and tunnels—the closest thing to solitary confinement Mother Nature had invented.

A Neanderthal scratched a bearded chin, regarding his superior wearily. "She is, boss ... but's she's dead. Died a couple hours ago."

Chapter Four

It was just under three hours ago that lead chemical biologist Jeffrey Laines had watched Captain Rice Sterling put a bullet in the temple of Commander Randall Stiessman's head and throw him from the chopper into the ocean. Watching Sterling pilot that same chopper while occasionally studying beeping radar screens, Laines wondered what the hell he had gotten himself into. Sure, Laines wanted the accolades for Project Nobleman. Sure, he wanted P-744 to be more his brainchild than Doctor Stan Imes's. Sure, Laines had agreed to oust Imes from his prominence as lead chemical biologist. But killing Stiessman hadn't been a part of it. No. Sterling hadn't made Laines privy to his private agenda to relieve Stiessman of his command in a most unsavory fashion and take control of 6,000 troops currently stationed in the region.

"An accident" was how Sterling had explained Stiessman's death to high-ranking officers aboard an aircraft carrier awaiting orders from their commander in the wake of the deadly tsunami. And, fearing for his life, Laines had backed up the story.

But now that Laines thought about it, there were a few things Sterling had neglected to tell him: the growing unrest, nervousness and uncertainty of the North Koreans over the US and Canadian military decision to test nuclear bombs and bio-chemical weapons on its own populace, all in the name of creating the perfect warriors. Wipe them out, infect them, create deviants who could then be killed by the subservient gladiators, not to mention The Neanderthals, whose extermination could be justified; they were just a malignant cancer.

Until recently, Laines had no idea that integral to the implementation of Project Nobleman, innocent civilians would be killed, infected, poked, prodded and abused like laboratory animals.

Never mind the rhesus monkeys, he thought, rubbing the scars on his cheek, a permanent and ugly reminder of the violent side effects of P-744. Under the influence of the drug, an out-of-control lab monkey had attacked Laines, raking sharp claws down his face, falling just short of clawing eyes from sockets and blinding him.

But that was the least of his problems right now. After Sterling executed Stiessman and ordered a missile strike on the escaping black submarine (piloted by Doctor Imes and containing Velvet and Nathan), the new commander casually informed Laines that the North Koreans had dropped a large non-nuclear bomb into the ocean, creating the tsunami wave that had obliterated District 101. Since gale-force winds and fierce storms had blown much of the poisonous radiation from the Canadian and American nukes over North Korea, the country's leaders weren't exactly enamored with the effort. At least that's what Laines was told. That, and Project Nobleman interfered with the North Korean nuclear program and its efforts to create super warriors.

As the chopper approached the deck of the large aircraft carrier, Laines questioned Sterling about how he knew it was the North Koreans who had decimated District 101; and whether the joint Canadian and American forces were in danger of being attacked a second time.

But Sterling seemed to realize the slip of tongue and had grown tight-lipped to Laines's subtle probing. "For now we're safe," Sterling had said, avoiding eye contact. Between the lines, there was the suggestion Sterling knew a lot more than he was letting on, even that he was in cahoots with the North Koreans.

That meant what Laines had long suspected. That Sterling not only had a precarious grip on sanity, but that his secret agenda evidently meant anyone who got in his way—including himself, Laines thought, shuddering—was expendable.

Laines wiped a sweaty brow and stared at a pulsating vein in Sterling's neck. Sterling pointed to a red pulsating dot on the blue radar screen and turned to Laines, who knew Sterling was pinpointing a building in Georgetown that had recently been bombed by Canadian military choppers in search of the wanted District 101 escapees.

"Did we get them?" Laines asked.

Sterling scratched a clean-shaven chin. The bulbous vein in his neck throbbed, slowly enlarging. "It looks like it, but I can't be sure."

"Didn't you just say the entire building was destroyed, not to mention fifty feet around it?" Laines asked, folding hands together to conceal nervousness.

"That's right. But I want to be sure." Sterling studied Laines for a few seconds. "You're sweating," he said finally, pointing to a tiny clear liquid ball rolling down the young doctor's forehead. "Is something wrong?"

"No," Laines lied, quickly wiping it off the tip of his nose. Something was wrong. He had just barely survived a massive deliberate tsunami wave initiated by the North Koreans, he had no idea when another gigantic and deadly wall of water might be forthcoming, and he was in a chopper with a wacko. "I'm just relieved to be on the bright side of the dirt—or in this case, the water."

Sterling grinned. "You stick with me, you'll stay on the bright side of the dirt."

"I plan on doing just that, sir," Laines said. He wasn't above ass-kissing, especially when it involved the preservation of his life.

Sterling's expression hardened. "What, stick with me or stay on the bright side of the dirt?"

"Both," Laines said as the chopper touched down amid stormy seas, swirling winds and darkening skies.

Sterling turned to Laines as two uniformed soldiers prepared to open the chopper doors. His dark eyes bored into him. "You're with me, right, Laines?"

"Of course," Laines said as a cold chill prickled up his spine. He thought he saw—no, *knew* he saw—dementia in the cold eyes of Commander Rice Sterling.

"You know those twenty-three trained warriors we got off District 101?"

"Yes sir," Laines said, pointing below deck as they climbed from the chopper. "They're in dorms, resting. I think it's going to take some time to get them ready, if that's what you want."

An approaching soldier began speaking and Sterling swatted the air in front of him like one might swat at a fly. "I'll deal with you in my office," he snapped. The soldier offered a feeble salute, turned, and left.

Sterling glared at Laines. "How much time?"

"I'd like to run some tests, see if we can correct some of the problems Imes created—"

"You have two days," Sterling said with a note of finality. "I want them ready for a mission by Friday."

Laines didn't have to ask what mission. He knew Sterling wanted them to search, locate, and destroy Velvet, Nathan, and Imes (if they were still alive), and see how many Neanderthals they could kill in the process.

"Friday?" Laines asked, biting his tongue as soon as he let the question slip.

"Is there an echo on this ship?" Sterling asked.

Laines looked at Sterling blankly.

"Friday morning at zero-seven-hundred hours, I want them battle-ready for a mission to PEI," Sterling said. And then in an uncharacteristically buddy-like tone, and with an enthusiastic shit-eating grin that Laines had never before seen etched into the commander's clean-cut features, Sterling added: "Show me what you can do, Jeff. And we'll conquer the world together."

Then Sterling's features hardened again and, dismissing Laines with an effective fly-swatting wave, said: "I've got work to do. Give me an update tomorrow at sixteen-hundred hours."

A few minutes later, in the privacy of his cabin, after he had caught his breath and manually pushed his racing heart back down from his esophagus to its normal operating position just behind and slightly left of the breastbone, Laines thought, *I'd like to give you something else tomorrow at sixteen-hundred hours ... fuckin' nutcase ... like an altered dosage of P-744 that would turn your psychotic mind into play-dough for a child ... fuck with a chemical biologist, you play with Doctor Death.*

Chapter Five

Less than thirty miles away, Nathan was having another enlightening experience with his version of Doctor Death, or Doctor-Life-In-The-Second-Realm as he would have preferred to call him. Two hours after the lust-filled carnal encounter with a near-insatiable Velvet Jones, to honor what he had considered to be the politically correct rules of Mary Anne Sole's household, Nathan had crept as quietly as a mouse back to his appointed room and settled into the wooden-framed cot beside the moonless window. After much joyful reflection on the fornication-filled recent events, particularly on the number of sexual positions they had tried—at least a third of the sixty-four detailed in the Kama Sutra—Nathan finally felt sleep tugging at his consciousness. Aided by counting imaginary breasts of all shapes and sizes—not sheep, as some might have preferred to count—exhaustion finally won the battle and swept Nathan dreamily to Never-Never Land.

It was there, in a surreal environment glowing radiantly with yellow light, that Edward Sole awaited his arrival. Unlike the last mind-altering encounter with Ed, they weren't in a dark, dank cave anymore. And there wasn't a torrent of deadly water washing Nathan violently down a path of what appeared to be imminent destruction, only to come out the other side and bear epiphanic witness to an all-encompassing, soul-suffusing yellow light, a fast-rewind review of his past, and then the inexplicable knowledge that somehow we don't really die. That we indeed pass on to the Second Realm, a realm perhaps much more satisfying and meaningful than any experience in the so-called real world.

In a deep sleep, Nathan, jaw-dropped, stared at the image of Ed. In the powerful yellow light, he could barely discern the features of his friend, his protector, and now maybe spiritual advisor. Then slowly the features became clear. Gone was the war paint. Gone were the demented eyes. Instead the eyes, large and oval, glowed fiery red in stark contrast to the calming body-and-mind-suffusing yellow hue that permeating the scene. Ed was draped in an ornate, gold-studded white robe and sat on a yellow throne that blended almost perfectly with the surrounding light. Nothing else was discernible.

"I'm back," Nathan said. "You're back."

"You're back because there are things you need to know," Ed said. He was stolid, impassive. Gone was the maniacal grin.

Indeed there were things Nathan wanted to know, perhaps needed to know. From the very first moment he saw Ed in the afterlife, when, at that time he didn't know it was Ed, he was told he was going to die painfully very soon. He wanted details, even if one part of him was beginning to embrace the conventionally-held concept of death. But Ed had said something else. "*You don't die, you just pass onto to another realm.*" What about that?

Nathan stood on what appeared to be a misty yellow cloud. The surface beneath him felt spongy, yet somehow secure. He addressed the transformed version of Edward Sole. "I want to know a few things ... like when am I going to die, and how?"

"You know when I lived in your realm, if someone would have said anything to me about God or spirituality I would have balked, probably would have knocked them off my friendship list and written them off as bible thumpers," Ed said. "But now I'm beginning to understand a few things ... not necessarily about God, but about spirituality and the Second Realm ... that if you believe in this realm it becomes your reality very quickly. But, if you don't believe, you'll never find it. Your death will be finite, blackness, nothingness, the end."

Nathan began questioning his own beliefs. He realized that in his entire lifetime, he hadn't given it a whole lot of thought. Maybe he had a vague spirituality, but had never really thought about it long enough to define it. Was he agnostic, believing in a higher power but, without sufficient proof, unable to attach it to any specific religious denomination? Perhaps, he thought, his mind returning to his death, when would it come, and just how painful would it be? A question, he realized grimly, that need not be answered. Maybe the answer would only bring forth gloom, doom, and a deep, hopeless despair. God knew he was having problems now staying upbeat in this Godforsaken hellhole of a world he had been thrust into. But, like a grieving spouse insistent on knowing the tragic details of his wife's violent murder, he pressed on. Ed, after all, seemed to be ignoring the question.

"I don't know about any of this spirituality stuff," Nathan said, realizing for the first time that maybe he wanted the answer so he could try and change his fate. "But I'd like to know when and how I'll die. And can I change it ... prevent it?"

"We'll get to that," Ed said, after a moment's pause. "You know during my life on PEI, I went through a really bad patch, came near the brink of suicide. I all but lost faith in the human race. I was drinking heavily, drunk-dialing and drunk-texting people; almost everyone blew me off. And I probably deserved it. But not you, Nathan, not you. And you know who else didn't blow me off?"

Nathan decided, at least for the time being, to leave the question of his fate alone. He thought, in his surreptitious style of pontification, Ed would get there soon enough. "Your grandmother, Mary Anne?" It was an educated guess. He saw the affection in Mary Anne's eyes when she spoke of her grandson.

"That's right. That woman's as solid as a rock. She gave me faith in humanity, gave me a reason to live. You and Cadence also played a small part in my recovery, and for that I would like to thank you."

"Not a problem. Is this leading somewhere?"

"I want you to take Mary Anne with you to Doctor Stan Imes's laboratory in Montague. If she stays in Georgetown she'll die very soon. She's been very brave with the fight. But she's not well and is going to die soon. Can you take her with you? Can you do that?"

Nathan didn't see how he was in a position to argue with a man who had done an amazing metamorphosis into someone approximating the Dalai Lama. Of course, he had other reasons for staying on Ed's good side. He wanted information, wanted time to process how that information would change his actions. Wanted to know if he had the intestinal fortitude to surrender—and possibly join Cadence, presumably in the Second Realm—or fight it. "I'll do it. But I can't hog-tie her if she resists."

"Don't worry. She'll come."

"What about me?" Nathan asked, growing exasperated.

After a short pause, Ed said, "You'll know once you get Mary Anne to the Second Realm, where she belongs."

"Wait a minute," Nathan said. He felt his fists clenching and was powerless to control them. "I'm not one of your prophets, Ed. I want to know what the fuck is going to happen to me. Maybe I don't give a shit about the life I have anymore, but I'd like to be able to decide that." He felt a ball of anger in the pit of his stomach, writhing its way upward like an angry serpent. Part of him wondered if it was the effects of P-744 and another part of him didn't care anymore. He felt a hot flush chase across his face. "Maybe I'll just surrender to this fate, but I want to know what it is. Don't bring these things up if you plan on leaving them open-ended ..."

Ed had disappeared and the surreal landscape had morphed from calming yellow to bleak blackness, as if his moods had the power to change surrounding colors. "Ed ... where did you go? Ed, come back. I'm sorry. Let's talk about this."

He stepped forward and slipped off the edge of a precipice, falling rapidly downward through the abyss—arms and legs outstretched—like a crashing airplane. Cold terror replaced the angry serpent. Falling, falling, falling, a fate unknown. He tried to scream. No sound came.

With rising panic, he realized he wasn't even exhaling ... he wasn't breathing. Maybe the end had come early and the pain was only a few seconds away. Maybe, like the unfortunate Wile E. Coyote in one of many botched attempts to capture the elusive roadrunner, he had splatted into the ground. Except unlike the cartoon, he wouldn't be able to pick himself up, dust himself off, and continue with the singular destructive goal that preoccupied the mind of Wile E.

With no breath and no words, Nathan felt his body tense, catatonic. Was rigor mortis setting in? *No,* he thought. *I don't want to die. I don't want to die. I changed my mind, Ed. Please, help me.*

Chapter Six

When Velvet heard the cry for help echoing in the hallway, her first reaction was to assume Nathan was just having a bad nightmare. Leave well enough alone. Besides, he had been acting a little weird lately—saw the light, visited another realm, apparently—and she wasn't sure how, over the long term, P-744 was going to manifest itself in Nathan. He had admitted to having murderous thoughts about her, although she had to admit the same thoughts were spiraling around her mind, disastrous side effects from P-744, she was sure. And, even though she was reticent to acknowledge it, there were other things, solid psychological walls, blocking her path to his door. Velvet had trust issues with men, aided and abetted by her low-life, abusive, pedophiliac father Jeritt and her scum-sucking, bottom-feeding, waste-of-space ex-boyfriend Eric.

She attributed her unusually sexually suggestive banter with Imes recently as nothing more than the love component of P-744. For better or worse, and the latter was the more accurate assessment, she was genetically modified, biologically different now. Only time would tell how the P-744 would change her perceptions, but she pinned some hope on Imes being able to reverse the effects and bring her back to what was maybe far from normal in others' eyes, but perfectly normal in her eyes. Cautious, weary, slow to trust, but a survivor and an independent one at that. Better to err on the side of caution, she thought, than unconditionally throw your trust to someone only to have them remorselessly squash it into the pavement like a pesky fly.

But there was something else bothering Velvet, something else preventing her from going to Nathan's aid. She noticed—and it was more than just the P-744-induced sexual encounters—there was a new energy between them, a new respect and fondness. She could see it in the way Nathan's green eyes regarded her, lingering a few moments longer than necessary during conversations, occasionally undressing her with his eyes. At first she had written it off as nothing more than just P-744 working its "magic," but lately she had started to question that hypothesis. The horniness brought on by the drug had its cycles. And typically, when she was feeling like fornicating with a bedpost, so was he. But these appreciative glances from Nathan were also occurring at intervals when the cyclic sex-inducing effects of P-744 were not apparent.

And, she too, felt her gaze lingering a little longer on Nathan. Was she falling in love with him? Was he falling in love with her?

Don't be ridiculous. Nathan's a man. Men always have sex on their minds. So maybe it was nothing more than that. Maybe she was reading too much into it, she decided, tossing on the bed as another "Help me, please" echoed eerily into the hallway. Maybe her woman's intuition was all wacked out.

She stopped tossing and another thought invaded her mind like an uninvited guest. *He saved your life. How bad can he be?* "Yeah, but I saved his, too ... I don't owe him shit," she said, putting her forefinger to her lips realizing she had spoken out loud. *You need him, idiot. You need alliances if you're going to have any chance of surviving this nightmare.*

That decided it. She had justified it in her mind. She was doing it for survival, out of a necessity to extend trust to those on her side. God knew, there were enough malignant forces to contend with, and she hadn't even begun to think about zombies, mutant birds, and what Doctor Imes had explained as a perfect climate for insects to grow, mutate, and turn violent—turn the tables after thousands of years of annihilation at unthinking human hands.

In the blackness, she slipped on a white t-shirt and blue jeans. For good measure she put on her steel-toed, steel-shanked combat boots, tucked her handgun into the crotch of her jeans, opened a squeaky door, and crept stealthily down the hall. It's not like she was waking up in the middle of the night in an idyllic and harmonious household, in an idyllic and peaceful life, to merely answer Mother Nature's call.

She arrived at Nathan's bedroom door, put her ear to it, and listened quietly. The sporadic light snoring of Mary Anne further down the hall was all she heard. She turned the doorknob and the door creaked open. Her eyes slowly adjusted to the dim orange glare reflecting in from the window painting lines across the rumpled blankets. Her jaw dropped open. She rubbed her eyes and did a double-take: pillows and blankets on the bed, but no Nathan.

Adrenaline coursed through her veins like hot molten lava as she quickly searched the entire room. She cautiously opened a small closet, starting and drawing her gun as a precariously hanging t-shirt slipped off a hanger and drifted to the floor. She spun around, ran down the hall, and pounded on Imes's door four times. Nothing. She pushed it open and had to squint at the blinding white light.

"What are you doing here?" Imes said, sitting up in bed, pointing a flashlight.

"Get that thing out of my eyes," Velvet said. "Nathan's gone."

Imes rubbed sleepy eyes and trained the beam on the floor. "What?"

"Nathan's gone. Get off your ass and help me find him."

"I'm coming," he said, slowly rising and fumbling around on a small night table for his clothes.

Velvet snatched his flashlight, spun around and headed for the door. "Meet me in Nathan's room," she said as she left. "I think I'm losing my mind."

Velvet walked briskly down the hall, reached Nathan's ajar bedroom door, entered, and shone the light on the bed. She sighed deeply. *Am I going nuts?* There he was, curled up in a fetal position. She moved closer, shining the small beam on his face. She knelt down to get a better look. His eyes were pressed tightly together and he was grimacing, as if bracing for a fall. She felt for a pulse.

There wasn't one.

She put her fingers gently to his nose, realizing with rising panic there was no air coming out his nostrils.

"Imes, get your ass in here," she yelled. "He's not breathing."

"Nathan," she said, beginning mouth-to-mouth resuscitation. "Wake up."

Imes appeared behind her. "Hold up," he said. "I'll do it."

Velvet stepped aside.

Imes bent down, realized quickly there was no pulse, tilted Nathan's head back, pinched his nostrils, and started breathing into Nathan's lungs.

A moment later, Nathan's eyes popped wide open. The grimace morphed to a look of fear, and he swung a well-aimed roundhouse punch that caught Imes in the side of the head with a thwack.

Imes's head jerked back and he crumpled to the floor. A one-punch knockout, and a sucker punch to boot.

Velvet stepped forward quickly, grabbing Nathan's other spasmodically jerking arm. His breath came in quick, panicked gasps.

"Nathan, it's me. Velvet. What's wrong with you?"

She felt his left arm relax and a look of terror swept across his face.

******

As Nathan slowly swam out of the deepest levels of unconsciousness, actually death, Imes's face had initially appeared to him as a demon: blood-red, with purple pulsating veins spider-webbed across his face. Imes's eyes appeared as black slits and a black, slithery serpent's tongue darted from elongated, clown-like, purple grinning lips. The doctor's arms were outstretched in Nathan's altered perception, hands with crooked, wickedly sharp six-inch nails reaching for his throat.

The punch came out of nowhere, reflexively, and after Nathan saw the doctor hit the floor, he realized it. He had just knocked out Doctor Imes. Velvet clung firmly to the other fist, which he realized painfully had been on its way to round-house punch her.

He coughed a few times and thought: *If that's the Second Realm, I want no part of it. It was just a nightmare, buddy, no different than the ones you've been having all your life.* Velvet stared at him, her face tight with concern. There was another look that Nathan couldn't quite decipher, something resembling incredulity, but he couldn't be sure. He was certain of one thing, though. He didn't want to say anything about seeing the light, the Second Realm, or any of that *stuff* that he now tried to convince himself was no more than a genetically modified mind gone haywire.

"Sorry," he said, after catching his breath. "It was just a bad nightmare, that's all." Her grip loosened on his wrist. "You can let me go. I'm not going to hit you."

Her grip tightened. "You sure?"

"Of course I am." But he was no more certain of the veracity of his words than he was sure that the sun would rise tomorrow.

She let go of his arm and Nathan looked at Imes, who lay face-first on the hardwood floor with his tongue hanging out.

"Is he okay?" Nathan asked.

Velvet shone the flashlight on Imes. Little droplets of spittle were leaking out of his mouth, snaking down his face and onto the floor. "You knocked him out," she said.

"It was an accident. I thought he was the Devil or something."

"Maybe he is. Look what he's done to us."

"Yeah, but right now he's our only chance of becoming normal again."

"I don't think we'll ever be normal again. Should we help him?"

Nathan nodded, and together they dragged Imes onto the bed.

The roar of a revving engine sounded outside.

"Get yer ass in gear. We've got company," Mary Anne shouted. She stood at the open bedroom door. In her emaciated state, she had risen to the challenge. She held an AK-47 assault rifle, a bullet belt was slung around her shoulder, and three hand grenades were strapped to a black belt that looked anomalous against red and white polka dot pajama bottoms. She'd had a chance to arm herself for battle, but evidently not enough time to slip into battle attire. But the look of determination, focus and resolve in her steel gray eyes said she didn't give a shit about battle dress protocol, if there were such a thing. She wanted to kill Neanderthals.

Nathan stared blankly at her, still stupefied by his journey into the Second Realm. Velvet stood behind him.

Mary Anne pointed down the hallway. "Get yerself some guns and start fighting. You wanna live forever?"

Nathan hurriedly dressed and rushed to the arsenal of weapons. Velvet was frantically arming herself and Nathan followed suit.

Mary Anne walked calmly into a bedroom and approached a window. She opened it and tossed a hand grenade out. A loud explosion rocked the two-story house. "I damaged their vehicle," she said, "but they'll be coming in any second now."

Velvet and Nathan were now both armed. Velvet slipped into commander mode. It seemed to come naturally, P-744 or no P-744. "Go wake up Imes and cover the main floor," she said, entering the bedroom where Mary Anne was now crouched by the window, picking off incoming enemies.

Nathan spun around, ran down the hallway and entered the bedroom where he had knocked Imes unconscious. Imes was bleary-eyed, just coming to. "What happened?" Imes said.

"No time for that," Nathan said, pulling him to his feet and handing him a machine gun. "We're under fire."

Imes's unfocused brown eyes became remarkably clear remarkably fast.

The cracking sound of wood splintering came from below. The Neanderthals were coming in through the front door. "I'm going down," Nathan said. "Cover me."

Another loud explosion shook the house and Velvet shouted, "Got you, you fuckin' pigs!"

Nathan arrived at the upper stair landing to a spray of machine-gun fire. A pattern of bullets dug into the wall behind him in an almost perfect pyramid shape.

Imes, now behind Nathan, sprayed bullets into the ceiling and white dusty chunks of plaster fell on Nathan's head. Nathan turned to Imes. "I said cover fire, not cover me with fire."

"Sorry," Imes said.

They ducked as another spray of bullets crunched into the plaster wall, this time in a V-pattern.

A little voice inside Nathan's head clamored for attention. *We don't die. We pass onto the other side.* It caused him to summon courage reserves he never would have given himself credit for. *Fuck the whole thing. I changed my mind. I do want to go to the Second Realm.*

He picked himself off the floor, stepped over a prostate, hands-protecting-head Imes, went to the landing and descended the stairs and into a hail of gunfire.

******

Velvet saw the pick-up truck explode and burst into flames. She hoped it contained occupants. She thought she saw a black silhouette trying to escape and then melting into the fiery haze, but she couldn't be sure. At something approximating four in the morning, the sky was dark and natural light had not come to visit the planet. The sun had not risen yet. There were no longer any guarantees with Mother Nature. Hell hath no fury like Mother Nature scorned. The figurative keeper of the planet's ecological balance had every reason to be as angry as an alcoholic who has just had his last 26-ounce bottle of whiskey flushed down the toilet.

But there was another thought more pressing in Velvet's mind. Watching Mary Anne's eyes, crazed and seemingly demented, as she fired rapidly into blackness, Velvet wondered if they had just blown up their only way out. Had the ticket to ride just expired? Then she heard the battle raging below. She accidentally grabbed Mary Anne's injured shoulder a bit too forcefully and said, "We need to get out of here. You have a vehicle?"

Mary Anne winced and stopped shooting. Her look of killer resolve faded, but only slightly. "In the rear garage. There's an old truck."

"Does it run?"

"Dunno. Used to."

"We have to go," Velvet said.

"This is my deathbed," Mary Anne said. "I'm not leaving. You go."

"No." Velvet grabbed her trigger hand as Mary Anne repositioned herself to continue firing. "You're coming with me."

******

Nathan heard a horrifying scream and then nothing as he descended the stairs. Then he saw another body—no, two bodies—dash down the hallway and into the living room directly below him. He pointed his machine gun at the stairs, riddling the steps with bullets. Then he poked the gun nozzle into the resulting hole, firing at what he could not see and hoping there were enemies below receiving unwelcome but powerful smooches of death.

"Fuck sakes, I'm hit," came a voice from below and Nathan smiled, unaffected by the pained cries of the enemy, their death, or his own for that matter. He was a Japanese kamikaze pilot readying himself for one last liberating, fateful blow to the enemy and a trip to the Second Realm for himself. This realm, at least for the time being, no longer held his interest; interest, perhaps, but willingness to exist in, no.

"Nathan," Velvet shouted from atop the stairs. "Go out front."

Nathan stopped firing long enough to see Velvet descending the stairs and Mary Anne disappearing down the upper hall toward the back of the house. Was there a second-floor fire escape out the back? Nathan wondered. But it didn't matter anymore. "I'm going to the Second Realm," he said, forgetting about his promise to Edward Sole to get Mary

Anne to Imes's secret underground laboratory in Montague. *Did I even promise that?*

With wild eyes, Nathan, on the main floor now, fired into the living room. He didn't even bother ducking or looking, just fired and fired and fired.

Velvet reached the main floor and crouched behind him.

A bomb blew a hole in the ceiling above the living room and the resulting shock wave catapulted Nathan and Velvet out the front door and onto a debris-strewn and flaming front lawn.

Nathan wiped dust from his eyes and, picking himself out of the debris, realized the steady thumping he heard was something other than the ringing in his ears from the bomb blast. Choppers were landing, genetically modified super soldiers were dispersing; soldiers sent by Commander Rice Sterling to seek and destroy Neanderthals and the would-be revolutionaries.

Mary Anne, driving a red pick-up, skidded to a stop in front of them. Doctor Imes climbed out of the passenger seat and ran to their aid. It seemed the doctor had found some courage after all, doing a 180-degree turn from his cowardly fetal-position crouch atop the stairs earlier.

Through blurred vision, Nathan saw Imes help Velvet to her feet. He thought about facing the troops head-on and going down in a blaze of gunfire and glory, which would lend significance to the Japanese kamikaze metaphor.

He didn't know why, probably never would, but Mary Anne's words changed his mind. "Don't even think about it," she said, rolling down the window. She had surprising reserves—piss and vinegar, some say—considering her years. "Get up and get yer ass in this truck. Now!"

Through unclear vision filled with peripheral purple and yellow dots expanding and contracting, Nathan staggered toward the truck. Imes had already tucked a dazed and confused black-from-bomb-blast-ash Velvet into the crew-cab. He held his hand out and the door open for Nathan.

Nathan reached the hand and felt a surprisingly strong grasp pull him inside.

"Fire this fuckin' thing," Mary Anne said to Imes, handing him an AK-47. She pointed the vehicle down a black alley and accelerated.

Troops filed out of a landed chopper and began firing.

The newfound courage was evidently still with Doctor Imes. Without hesitation, he stuck the gun out an open window, looked back, and opened fire. Nathan and Velvet were sitting in the back seat, heads lolling to and fro like punch-drunk string-puppets.

Another chopper landed and a Humvee rolled out, beginning pursuit.

Headlights behind them loomed larger.

"We've got company," Imes said. "Step on it."

"Don't worry," Mary Anne said. "I know where to go where they won't follow."

Nathan's head began to clear and he glanced over at Velvet. She looked barely conscious and had a two-inch cut on her forehead, oozing blood into her eye and down her face. Nathan used his shirtsleeve to wipe the blood away as the pick-up truck made a series of quick turns, bouncing along the bumpy back alley.

Imes continued firing into headlights of death.

"You're cut," Nathan said, staring at the blood on his sleeve. Velvet had only just removed the white gauze from the previous cut, replacing it with a combination of smaller adhesive bandages.

"I'm ... I'll be okay," Velvet said, putting a hand to a growing goose egg above the gash. "What were you thinking back there?"

"Hold on to your seats," Mary Anne shouted, fish-tailing the truck hard right and finding traction on what looked like a driveway.

Lit up by explosions, and perhaps Mother Nature's promise of a sunrise, the sky had turned a dim orange-gray color. At the end of the 150-foot driveway, small dancing white lights buzzed, the sound growing louder.

"Where are we going?" Nathan asked.

"Just hold on," Mary Anne said, "... only one shot at this."

Imes had stopped firing and was staring grimly at the spectacle of intricate webbing now coming into view. "Oh my god," he said. "I knew it."

Mary Anne zigzagged, straightened the wheel, and floored the pick-up. It bounced up a mound of dirt and sprang airborne for a split-second before landing roughly in an intricate network of webs. Mary Anne backed up, slammed it into drive, and accelerated. The rear wheels were getting no traction, spinning dirt, gravel and debris.

Nathan looked behind and saw it: a brilliant red hourglass shape against a shiny black round abdomen, eight gigantic claw-tipped legs, four glowing red eyes and gigantic jagged jaws nearing.

A black widow spider, spanning maybe fifty feet, closed in for the kill.

In spite of his death wish, Nathan couldn't help feeling the tiny hairs on his back and neck turn cold and a black ball of terror begin to well up in the empty pit of his stomach. *My God. The tables have turned.* "It's a fucking black widow," Nathan said as rear tires continued spinning on loose dirt, tangled webbing and debris. He wondered now why the spider was one of his favorite arachnids.

The monstrous arachnid quickly closed the gap, descending on its prey with rapid and efficient precision. Large jaws of death opened directly above the vehicle and giant yellow retractable fangs slowly emerged, dripping with black, deadly poison.

But an engine noise behind diverted the genus Latrodectus. It spun around and quickly doused an airborne incoming Humvee with a large tangled mass of webbing that trapped it in its tracks. A soldier, head sticking out the open cab top, trained an assault rifle on the spider and prepared to open fire. But the creature was instantly upon the Humvee. Retractable fangs extended with lightning speed, decapitating the attacker. Spewing blood like a cold-water tap, horrifying screams echoed from the mouth of the helmeted head that flew through the air, landing with a hollow thud on the ground below.

Another soldier stuck his gun out an open window. He got off a short burst, ripping into one of the black widow's legs, before a retractable fang severed his arm—like a sharpened butcher knife through medium rare roast beef—at the shoulder.

And as the soldier screamed in pain, Nathan, for the moment, witnessed no more carnage and bloodshed in the new world order. The tires of the pick-up truck, as if by divine intervention, miraculously found traction, bit into dirt and lurched forward.

Imes pointed the gun out the window as Mary Anne guided the vehicle down a dark, winding road marked by dead and menacingly overhanging trees. "Put that thing inside," she shouted. "He's not a threat to us anymore."

Imes obeyed.

Terrifying cries of death grew fainter, marking their progress away from the black widow's lair.

Mary Anne stopped the truck under cover of a demolished house and put it in park. She rubbed a hand over her wounded and bandaged shoulder. "I'm tired and sore. Anyone else fit to drive?" She looked at Imes, who stared at her horrified for a few seconds before finally nodding.

Nathan listened. But for faint chopper rotors and hissing winds blowing decaying trees, all was silent. He looked again at Velvet, who held her hand to the goose egg on her head. "You okay?" he asked. Aided by the rush of adrenaline, he felt lucid now, the purple and yellow dots not quite gone from his periphery, but certainly forgotten.

She removed her hand from her head and examined her palm. The blood was sticky, beginning to coagulate.

"It's a small cut and a mild concussion," Imes said, opening the door and switching places with Mary Anne, whose movements had become slow and lethargic, as if her recent life-saving maneuvers had sapped what remained of her aging energy reserves.

"I'm fine," Velvet said. "Don't worry about me. You've all got better things to worry about. With giant spiders, I'm sure come giant flies."

Imes tried to give her a reassuring look, but failed dismally.

Nathan saw it in Imes's pained expression. This was only act one to a five-act tragedy. The man obviously knew much more than he was saying. But, too exhausted from the adrenaline infusion and subsequent crash, not to mention shock, he decided for now to leave well enough alone. Soon, he would learn about all the dangers and have an opportunity to revisit the notion of whether any of it really mattered to him anymore.

Besides, there was something else still coursing through his body—an emotion that with his new bravado and recklessness had evaded him of late. And that emotion was raw, cold fear. He had to admit, the narrow escape from the gigantic spider had brought him in tune with the fear factor like never before. A terrifying new world order was emerging, and it was anyone's guess where it would end.

As they drove along the deadwood road, an ominous gray-orange sky now looming overhead, Nathan grew quiet, lost in his thoughts. Mary Anne extracted a first-aid kit from the glove box, turned around and began slowly and methodically disinfecting and bandaging Velvet's injury.

Nathan thought about the giant spider, then about giant flies. They would come, he now felt sure, remembering how the pesky, disease-carrying insects ate; after scraping solid food into flakes—or in the case of a human, chunks of flesh—house flies vomit saliva and acidic digestive juices on the intended meal and wait for it to be broken down into a softer, more liquid state before dining.

His stomach lurched. What could he vomit on a near-empty stomach? He pushed the acidic puke ball down and tried to think of something more pleasant. But an unpleasant memory surfaced, a news story he had read about Mark Vogel, a thirty-something quirky man living in Germany who kept a zoo of lizards and insects in his apartment, many of which were not suitable for domestication, never mind captivity in a residence. Tampering with Mother Nature, Vogel learned his lesson the hard way. He was fatally bitten by a pet black widow spider and then eaten by the other creepy-crawlies.

Neighbors, alarmed by the foul smell coming from Vogel's apartment, alerted police, who discovered a nightmare scene: spiders, snakes, a gecko lizard and thousands of termites had gorged on his corpse. What remained of Vogel's body was found on a sofa with giant webs—some coming from his nose and mouth—draped over him. In a chilling and macabre scene that talented director David Cronenberg may have been hard-pressed to rival, police even discovered larger chunks of flesh, apparently torn off by the lizards, had been collected and taken to the webs of bird-eating spiders and tarantulas.

Recalling the gory details, and realizing with cold terror that they could meet their end in a similarly grisly fashion, Nathan shuddered and the puke ball lurched again.

"Stop," he said.

Travelling west through what used to be Brudenell River Provincial Park but was now a mess of angry decaying trees, Imes had arrived at a clearing, leading to Highway #3 west, which would take them to Highway #4 and then into

Montague, The Beautiful, as its welcome sign had once proudly proclaimed.

Imes stopped and glanced back at Nathan, whose face had turned jaundiced yellow. "Let me out. I think I'm going to be sick."

They did. He stepped out, went to the back of the vehicle, and puked a sticky yellow mixture. After a while, he was dry-heaving and coughing.

In a minute, Velvet was at his side, a comforting hand on his shoulder as he knelt down. "Are you okay?"

He stopped coughing. Everything was beginning to take a toll. "Am I supposed to be okay? We're not the same anymore ... modified into what ... who the fuck knows. The world has quite gone to shit, we've got spiders the size of barns out there, mutant animals and birds, fucking zombies, Neanderthals and a military controlled by megalomaniac psychos bent on our destruction. Oh, I'm sure I'm missing something, Velvet." Nathan's face was beet-red with frustration and anger. "Right, tsunami waves, manufactured by who the fuck knows, that for all we know could come crashing down any second and wipe us the fuck out ..." He cleared his throat and spit a gob of the remaining yellow puke. It stuck to a nearby decaying tree branch and dangled precariously, forming a perfect circle like a waiting hangman's noose.

Velvet stared at the dangling spittle for a few seconds. It fell from the branch and hit the ground with a barely audible splat. "You're scared."

Nathan's nausea was beginning to pass. He stared at her and, not for the first time, marveled at her resilience. In spite of all the terror and death, Velvet maintained a coat-of-armor front. There were very few chinks in the metal. Her traumatic upbringing and life experience had obviously taught her independence, self-reliance, and toughness. She had turned the tables on the victim role, instead learning how to survive—and yes, even thrive—in a stormy tide of chaos. Hell, she was probably at her best when things were at their absolute worst. She had become a master at putting her emotions in a steel chest buried deep in her heart and hiding the key, maybe even throwing it away.

"I thought my kamikaze act back at the house was the way to handle it, give up on this realm and hope against all hope the Second Realm really exists ... my way out of all this shit," Nathan said. "But sometimes my mind doubts the whole experience with Ed, won't believe it's real, and it drifts back to this shitty existence and how terrifying it really is. Then everything piles up and I get scared. Yes, scared and damned confused about everything."

Velvet's hand gently glided from the nape of Nathan's neck to his shoulder. She looked at him directly with those deep green eyes, a wave of affection and sympathy passing through pupils that seemed to be lit from the inside. Maybe Nathan was wrong about Velvet's ability to hide her emotions. He could see emotion all over her face now.

"It's okay to be scared," she said. "But fear is a mind-killer. You have to face it ... like you did before, but more controlled. Face it and overcome it. It's the only way."

******

Looking at the pitiful sight in front of her, the sad visage of a broken man, or one very near to shattering into a million pieces like a cursed and haunted mirror, Velvet couldn't help the pangs of sadness that permeated her heart. She didn't blame Nathan for feeling this way. When the spider had almost chomped them for breakfast, she too had felt tentacles of cold terror curl into a ball and rise up in her esophagus, coming very close to manifesting itself in projectile vomit. It was all she could do to swallow hard, three or four times, and force the insistently rising ball back into the pit of her stomach.

She released her hand from his shoulder as Nathan straightened his posture and wiped puke from his face and chin with a shirtsleeve. The look in his eyes was of utter hopelessness, confusion, fear and despair, all wrapped into one neat but heart-wrenching package. Maybe now was the time to tell him, she wondered.

Before she could process the thought properly, she blurted it out: "This morning, before you cold-cocked Imes, you disappeared."

"What?"

"You disappeared, Nathan. You went somewhere. I heard cries of help coming from your bedroom, checked on you, and you were gone. I woke Imes, came back, and you were there."

Confusion was the overriding emotion on Nathan's face now. "You mean I actually physically went somewhere?"

She nodded. "I don't know how, but unless I'm going nuts, I swear that's what happened." A slow realization entered Velvet's mind. Perhaps she shouldn't have blurted it out. Nathan might grow ever more anxious to enter the Second Realm. The recklessness she had seen in his eyes as he descended the steps of Mary Anne's house, shooting Neanderthals, was an abandon she had never before seen him possess—a complete disregard for his life; indeed, a Japanese fighter pilot going in for one last liberating death blow to the enemy.

She didn't approve of his reckless abandon. Nor did she approve of his Second Realm pursuit.

Why?

In a mind racing with multiple joined, disconnected and permanently frayed thoughts, it dawned on her. One, she was afraid of what she might find in the Second Realm, afraid she might see her father Jeritt, or her ex-boyfriend Eric, returning to haunt and abuse her some more. She didn't know if heaven or hell really existed. This was the only hell she knew, and it was a living hell. But she didn't want to think about it either, didn't want to drag up all those painful memories of abuse from the locked chest deep within a cavernous, dark and heretofore untouched area of her mind—a locked chest in a locked cave in a locked tunnel, the key not thrown away but mangled and twisted beyond usage, never to be reshaped into an instrument capable of opening doors meant to stay locked forever.

Two, she didn't want Nathan to go the Second Realm. She wanted him here, at her side. Right now, she had her doubts about Mary Anne, and definitely didn't fully trust Doctor Imes. Who else was there? In spite of the unpredictably scary—though some enjoyable, to be sure—effects of P-744, Nathan was the only one she trusted right now. Maybe not fully—you had to earn Velvet's trust, and continue to earn it—but enough to realize he was beginning to occupy a special place in her heart, a heart she had long since written off as incapable of anything remotely resembling true love.

A voice in Velvet's head began speaking. It was the same self-assured voice that had prevented her for many long, lonely years from engaging in committed affairs of the heart with members of the opposite sex. But the voice seemed to have lost some of its self-assuredness, resolve and influential force. *Don't be silly. It's the P-744. But is it?*

A weakening heart was alien to Velvet, and she didn't like it. Didn't like it one bit. Love made you vulnerable. And when you were vulnerable, you did silly, stupid things, things in this hostile environment that could make you very dead very fast. And she didn't want to get very dead very fast. She didn't know what she wanted, but she didn't want that. With tiny, invisible hands, she wrapped up the ball of emotion, took it into a dark cave in her mind, placed it in a steel chest alongside many others, padlocked it shut, and grimaced as she tried to bend the steel key to render it unusable.

******

For someone Nathan had thought was remarkably adept at hiding emotion, Velvet was displaying a range of emotions: fear, sadness, affection, and confidence, to name a few. He was about to write it off as merely P-744-induced psychosis—wasn't he slowly going stark-raving mad?—but the deep and palpable pain in Velvet's watery eyes was unlike any reaction he had ever seen before. She was changing and it had nothing to do with drugs, he thought. She was becoming sensitive, at least with him. This time it was Nathan who put a hand on Velvet's shoulder.

She recoiled at his touch. Sadness flashed across hardened eyes for a split-second, and then her brave warrior face emerged.

"Are you okay?" he asked.

The voice inside Velvet's head: *Everything's fine, Velvet. It always is when you don't wear your heart on your sleeve.* Later that night, she would ask herself why the voice, the voice of reason and self-preservation, had so abruptly abandoned her, and the answer would be as evasive as that of a politician accused of spying on his neighbors.

"No," she said. "I'm not okay. I don't want you to die."

Nathan stepped closer and hugged Velvet, hoping his recent vomiting episode, or her internal hard-wired self-preservation mechanism, wouldn't make her recoil again.

She didn't, instead melting into his embrace, wrapping her arms around him tightly, resting her head on his shoulder and softly kissing his neck.

For a very brief moment, everything was all right.

"Excuse me," Mary Anne said. She and Imes were watching them with the same interest a lonely singleton would display watching a young couple smooch in public. "Could we save the romance until we find Doctor Imes's lab?"

"The lab," Nathan said, remembering his recent out-of-body conversation with Ed. "In the Second Realm, Ed made me promise to get Mary Anne to the lab."

Mary Anne looked at Imes curiously. "Second Realm? Ed? What the hell is he talking about?"

Imes mustered his most convincing tone. "I have no idea."

Chapter Seven

"You have no idea what you're dealing with," Mary Anne said to Imes fifteen minutes later as he pulled off a debris-strewn Highway #4 and into Montague's Community Park Cemetery. Tilted, smashed, and overturned tombstones were poking up defiantly; crumbling monuments to a long-gone era.

"I know the lab's here," Imes said, maneuvering the vehicle slowly around stone markers for the dead.

"Last time I was here, this place was overrun with Neanderthals," Mary Anne said.

Nathan sat quietly with his thoughts. After the breakthrough with Velvet—yes, it was a real breakthrough—the pick-up was attacked by a military chopper. But this time, it was the insects, probably unwittingly, that had come to their defense.

They had just turned left onto Highway #4 when the chopper swooped down out of nowhere and began firing missiles, accompanied by bursts of machine-gun fire. Driving, Imes dodged and darted, narrowly avoiding incoming fire, when suddenly they heard a loud buzzing sound, so loud and eardrum-splitting that almost in unison, multiple hands covered multiple ears as the buzzing intensified. Nathan, who had recovered some of his faculties by that time, snatched up an AK-47, rolled down the window, aimed, and was about to fire when he witnessed an attack right out of a well-choreographed horror movie.

En masse, a swarm of hundreds of gigantic black flies descended on the chopper, clinging to it with such momentum and force they sent it spiraling end-over-end in mid-flight, then crash-landing and exploding into a ball of flames. And, as if by the same morbid curiosity that causes a black housefly to repeatedly crash into an illuminated incandescent light bulb and spin around until the heat from the light or the fly's repeated smashing—tick, tick, tick—causes its death, dozens of flies, apparently fascinated with the orange and red, black-smoked spiraling flame, buzzed around it, zeroing closer until flames licked, lapped, and sucked many of them down into a fiery death.

Kamikaze flies, Nathan thought, and he couldn't help smiling dumbly. Maybe he was going crazy? He had every reason to be.

"Get out and quit daydreaming," Mary Anne snapped.

Nathan refocused on the present, noticing Mary Anne, Velvet, and Imes standing outside the vehicle, staring at him like you might someone who is losing his marbles. Apparently he had just missed some conversation and a few priceless moments of time.

"Are we here?" Nathan asked, wiping his eyes as if that would instantly clear up his woes and make everything right again. The nausea might have passed, but a new feeling of semi-alertness—maybe semi-consciousness—was spreading body and mind-numbing tentacles through a biological system already reeling from yet-not-totally known side effects of P-744, not to mention a trauma-induced catatonia of sorts.

"We've been here for two minutes, Nathan," Velvet said pleadingly. "Snap out of it, will you? We need you sharp, not in a haze."

She extended a hand, which he graciously took and stepped out of the vehicle. As they slowly walked around the skeletal remains of what was once a thicket of bushes, they heard a faint buzzing in the distance, growing slowly but definitively louder.

Kamikaze flies or military choppers? Nathan thought. *Or maybe both.*

They followed Imes past demolished grave markers. He stopped at a round metal manhole cover.

"A sewer?" Velvet asked. "You're taking us into a sewer?"

Imes shook his head, an expression approaching a scowl flickering across and then disappearing from his face. "It's the lab. The location is secret. Remember?"

Imes knelt down, put his hand into a small hole beside the manhole cover, and twisted what appeared to be a metal doorknob of sorts. The metal cover creaked and snapped open. "It still works," he sighed. "Thank God for technology."

As they descended, Nathan couldn't resist one last look at the sooty gray, orange, and yellow sky. In the distance, he saw a chopper approaching. Then the buzzing intensified and the black swarm, en masse, attacked its new found prey. He shuddered, slammed the lid shut, and locked it. A thunderous boom rocked the metal ladder beneath his feet as the chopper crash-landed and exploded, not two hundred yards north.

Reaching the bottom of the twenty-foot ladder, Nathan stood in total blackness beside the others, expecting another dark and gloomy journey, one he wasn't sure he had the stomach for. *It's my party and I'll cry if I want to, cry if I want to, cry if I want to. You would cry too if it happened to you.* He didn't know why the lyric had popped into his head, and he doubted very much Lesley Gore—although her surname certainly implied it—had this horror in mind when her version of the song climbed to the top of music charts. No. The song tells of the discomfiture of a teenage girl who loses her love interest at her birthday party, not of a sickening journey through a post-apocalyptic wasteland.

Doubts began to creep into Nathan's mind; doubts about the reason for being here, doubts about Doctor Imes. *Are we really here to reverse P-744's effects?* Was that really what the good doctor had in mind, bringing them down here? Maybe the real horror was just about to start.

"Where's the lab?" Nathan heard himself ask, trying but failing to control rising panic in his voice. *Don't be a crybaby. Forget it. Kamikaze ... you're a Japanese kamikaze, and this is your last liberating mission. The Second Realm ... welcome it. No. Velvet? Cadence? Mary Anne. Ed. Fulfill your promise, numbskull. You were a lot of lousy things, but never a man who wasn't good for his word. Be good for your word. At least be good for that.*

Fluorescent lights flickered and illuminated, instantly turning black to white, blinding white. A sign, he thought. *Light at the end of the tunnel. Not a dark and gloomy journey like you imagined.* Nathan stared at Imes blankly. They stood in a narrow, white, sterile-looking corridor in front of an elevator with dusty stainless-steel doors. Nathan caught his distorted reflection in the doors and noticed what a state he was in. His crew-cut was beginning to grow out, unkempt. A grizzled gray-brown patchwork of facial hair partially concealed wincing lips, gaunt cheeks and chin. Green eyes, once clear and alert, were now hazy with fatigue and the dreamy faraway quality of the mentally-very-far-from-Earth.

"Good, the back-up generator still works," Imes said. Then, looking into Nathan's eyes as a doctor would study a patient not responding favorably to treatment, he frowned. "Three floors down. Don't worry. It's not a long trip." The right side of Imes's cheek and chin had turned a purple-black from Nathan's sucker-punch a few hours earlier. Occasionally he rubbed it. They entered and Imes pressed L. The elevator clunked, groaned and then began a slow wheezing descent, its protestations borne of idleness. It clanged to a stop at L, the sound reverberating metallically through the elevator shaft. The door opened.

"What are the other two floors?" Velvet asked as they stepped out of the elevator to a small lobby. Long, fluorescently lit corridors extended both ways.

"One is administration; two, research and development; and here, level three, is the lab where we produce the finished product," Imes said, pointing down the left corridor. "There are fully-equipped suites down there. First three doors on the left. Get some rest ... we'll meet in the lab in a couple of hours." Imes pointed right. "The lab's the third door down this corridor. The door's marked Project N."

Nathan might have had a concept of time when the world was "normal," but now, with no functioning watch, and a sunset not as consistent as death and divorce, he had lost touch with humankind's need to impose order on a reality that was as out-of-control as a brakeless speeding semi-truck. "How do I know when that is?" he asked.

"Don't worry," Imes said. "The communications are up. I'll buzz you." He caressed his swollen cheek. "And there are wall-clocks in all suites."

"There any food in this place?" Velvet asked as Imes turned to leave. "I'm starving."

"Vending machines down the hall," Imes said. "In the cafeteria. You'll find it. You may have to smash them to get anything."

"That's not a problem," Velvet assured him.

Imes left.

Mary Anne slumped against the wall and began sliding to the floor from fatigue. Nathan and Velvet each took an arm and helped her into a queen-sized bed in a utilitarian studio-suite down the hall. They laid her down gently and left. She was snoring by the time they closed the door.

"Quite a woman," Velvet said to Nathan, nodding to the closed door. "For her years, she's got the heart of a lion."

Nathan nodded and an uncomfortable silence followed.

"Wanna join me for a stale sandwich and a Coke?" Velvet asked finally, making brief eye contact before darting her green eyes to the gray floor tiles.

"I think I'll take a nap. Rough night last night."

"See you later. I want to talk to you later, though. In private." She turned and walked away.

Chapter Eight

Lying in bed, staring at blackness, a part of Nathan wanted to get as far away from this chaos as possible. Multiple dark thoughts, like disconnected pieces of a macabre jigsaw puzzle, spun around in his mind. For better or worse, he had fulfilled his promise to Edward Sole, delivered his grandmother to Imes's underground lab. Now would he meet his death as Ed had foretold? A grim, grisly and painful death? A peaceful, pain-free passing? Then what? Would he go to this Second Realm, connect and live happily ever after with Cadence, white-robed on a puffy white cloud far away from the madness on Earth? Maybe even have a puffy white picket fence? What was this Second Realm, where a certifiably psychotic—albeit heroic and good-hearted—Edward Sole could not only ascend to, but indeed become some kind of gatekeeper, proselytizer, even prophet?

And that was only the bottom of the anthill. There were his conflicted feelings about Velvet, the attraction to her that was becoming much more, he was sure, than the effects of P-744. That, juxtaposed with his need, desire, longing to be reunited with Cadence. *But I'll find out if Imes can reverse the effects of this fucked up drug, or whatever it is. Find out if the emotion for Velvet is real or fake.*

But he also had his doubts about Imes. Certainly the man had come to his rescue, but hadn't he been the man who also invented P-744? Could he really, fully, be trusted? Weren't megalomaniacs all the same? Eventually their egotistical nature, desire to order human behavior, create the perfect race—at least their vision of the perfect race—would override any genuine concern for humanity. And they would have a million reasons to justify their behavior. Collateral damage. Sacrifice a few for the greater good. If you want a peaceful, law-abiding, subservient culture, casualties are just part of the game. There would be rewards: accolades, trophies, the Nobel Peace Prize, recognition and admiration from peers.

But what had they created? Nathan shuddered as a collage of horrific images assaulted his soul: human-eating giant spiders; swarming, buzzing, enormous flies; ruthless Neanderthals; frothing, frenzied zombies; mutant, attacking seagulls; mutant, crazed pigs ...

It was all becoming too much for his overloaded psyche. "Stop," he said aloud. "Stop it, stop it, stop it all ..."

Nathan prayed for sleep to take him away from the chaos in the world, the chaos in his mind, the chaos in his soul. Sleep, permanent or impermanent, was the only answer, the only peace.

But he tossed and turned restlessly. And a small man crawling inside Nathan's mind walked into a deep, dark compartment of concealed memories, took a small key, and opened a door. Long-buried skeletons exploded from a closet. Memories he had tried to suppress, had been aided by the amnesia to do just that, flooded forth like a tidal wave. Without anything else to do, he struggled to make sense of them, learn something of who he really was.

He'd graduated with an English literature undergraduate degree from Simon Fraser University in Burnaby, British Columbia, just on the fringe of the cosmopolitan city of Vancouver, where he rented a small studio apartment. His first job—welcome to the trenches—had been gutting fish at a fish processing plant. He left after three months, securing a reporting job for *The Guardian*, a local paper in PEI. He wanted a more cerebral and independent existence away from the trappings and stresses of a big city.

But it was more than that. It was his father, Tom. Tom verbally abused Nathan—*You'll never amount to shit*—and was at times physically abusive: a hard backhand, the steel-tipped leather belt, once even a straight right to the eye followed by a left uppercut to the jaw. *Two-punch knock-out, boss. I don't think he's getting up.*

Tom was moody. If he was in a foul temper, often brought on by alcohol, but more often by a hangover, anything Nathan said would send him off. *"Dad, can I have some money to go to the store?"* Wham! *"Dad, can I go out and play?"* Wham! *"Dad, can my friend Wayne come over?"* Wham! *"Dad, don't hit Mom."* Wham! *"Dad, I said please don't hit Mom."* Wham! He learned to avoid his father like the plague, tiptoeing cautiously around his foul moods, which luckily averaged about three times a week (when Tom was in a good mood, he could actually be quite congenial and loving to his only son).

But soon, Nathan lost all respect for Tom. The conversations became less polite. They would be followed by a crash, but it was the crash of a door banging shut after Nathan had fled. *"Dad, did anyone ever tell you you're an asshole? No, well I'm telling you. You're a fucking asshole."* Crash! *"Dad, you say I won't amount to shit, but what have you amounted to? A wife-beating, son-beating, alcoholic loser."* Crash! Fortunately, Nathan could outrun his father. And by then he knew the man's temperament. He knew a few hours later, after he had returned home, Tom would forget all about the exchanges and a beating would not be forthcoming. Most times, anyway, but not all the time. Twice, at least twice that Nathan recalled, Tom had remembered the "disrespect" and Nathan had been strapped so badly with the steel-tipped belt, the cheeks of his ass were cut and bleeding, and he couldn't sit down for weeks.

He left Surrey, British Columbia, where he was born. Left the entire province, going from west coast to east coast, as far away from the trauma as possible at the time. BC might have been beautiful to some, but for Nathan it was a thick leather straitjacket of painful memories. He wanted to lose it and be free. No wonder he had blocked out images of his father, even his mother, who he supposed he still blamed for allowing him to suffer Tom's abuse and not press criminal charges.

But hadn't Anna, maybe out of some guilt she felt about subjecting her only son to Tom's abuse, not to mention the abuse she had suffered, gotten her revenge in the end? Forty-four fatal stab wounds later, Nathan supposed she had. Maybe it had been her way of apologizing to Nathan for not having the courage to stand up to him for so many years. He sighed. He would never know. She was dead now. At least with his mother, he had felt sorry for her. And, yes, he loved her.

The small man in his troubled mind reappeared, pushed the skeletal bones inside the closet, crammed the door closed, and left. A skull and a few arm bones protruded out, leaving the door slightly ajar.

With much sadness and pain, Nathan recapped, bone by haunting bone, the skeletons of his past.

Finally, he willed his mind to think of more pleasant memories; life on the Island, for example. After an hour, he found a measure of success.

PEI hadn't been an easy adjustment for Nathan. He didn't have a lot of friends, didn't find it easy to make friends. He knew the Island could be an awfully lonely place if you weren't firmly seeded into social groups. He had heard many of the local singles used the internet to find companionship, small isolated communities making easy and commute-free socializing difficult.

So he became introverted and absorbed by achieving success, probably just to spite Tom's convictions to the contrary. Tom probably didn't realize it at the time, but his criticism had the opposite effect on Nathan, inspiring him to succeed, become a better person, prove to himself that he would not grow up and be like the old man. So he worked hard, saved his money, bought rental properties and a waterfront wooded acreage near small-town Murray River (a property he liked to call PEI Paradise, but his vehicle GPS mispronounced as Pay Paradise).

He remembered the happy moments being outside in the forest, working around the property, repairing the 130-year-old Victorian-style two-story house, fixing the outbuildings, converting the barn to a garage, cutting through deadfall on the property—he thought the Stihl MS-341 chainsaw was the best man-toy ever invented by God—and particularly near his private beach, where he had cleared an old 2,000-ft road that led from house to beach. He wanted to clear a picturesque clearing from which to enjoy the beach, sunsets, wild animals, and birds. It was there, in the forest, on the beach, or working outside around the house and three outbuildings, where he found most of what he liked to call his Kodak moments; although often the only photos were mere mental images from which he found a certain inner peace while recollecting.

His last thought before finally drifting off was of cleaning out an outbuilding on PEI Paradise on a beautiful summer day.

As he drifted into lower levels of consciousness, the image transformed into a dream.

And it felt so damned real.

He was at his PEI property, pre-Cadence Whittaker union. He had just finished evicting some chipmunks from a bedroom-sized outbuilding, probably built before he was born. He smiled as he returned to the building with plywood, hammer and nails to seal off the holes in the floor where the critters had entered. *I'll get you, motherfuckers.* He had just removed a nest of leaves, shredded air mattresses, bits of paper and plastic, and tossed them into a blazing bonfire. The chipmunks, after all, had ripped to rat-shit three brand-new air-mattresses he had used *before,* for floating lazily on warm summer ocean waters, soaking up rays, and listening to gently lapping waves. Nathan was none too pleased when he first discovered the shredded remains of his summer-toys-slash-guest-beds.

Opening the door, a lone chipmunk regarded him quizzically, its head poking out from floorboard rot, squeaking and squawking—a scene right out of *Caddie Shack*—as much as to ask, "You mean I have to leave?"

Nathan stopped and stared at the little critter for a few seconds, feeling a moment of sympathy. Then he remembered the shredded air-mattresses. "Sorry, buddy, but you gotta go."

After sealing off the outbuilding, he returned to the blazing bonfire. He sat down smoking a cigarette and drinking a beer, reflecting on the nature of animals versus humans. The evicted chipmunk—Mugs, Nathan called him—only wanted a roof over his head.

But animals didn't cheat you. Animals didn't lie. Animals wouldn't tell you to fuck off, at least not in words you could understand. Animals wouldn't automatically give you their trust. You had to earn it. And after some time, and many peanuts, he had earned the trust and forgiveness of Mugs. The chipmunk visited Nathan occasionally, venturing out of the tree-line bordering the property and coming ever closer to the house with each visit. Sometimes Mugs would climb up Nathan's pant leg to an open hand containing peanuts, grab one with an out-stretched claw, scurry away and bury it, and then return for one or two more before disappearing to whatever was his daily ritual.

And then there was Robbie the Rabbit, a small, brown, crazy, and unpredictable creature, who once made a beeline for the open back door of Nathan's house after he had one day left it open, as if Robbie had a not-so-secret agenda to domesticate Nathan. But, unlike Mugs, Robbie wasn't as generous with his company. It had taken Nathan six months before he was finally able to get within thirty feet of Robbie, who would stare at Nathan curiously while slowly chewing on a blade of grass and then sucking the last few inches into his mouth as if it were a delicious lollipop. After a few minutes, he would high-tail it into the bush, disappearing behind the thick forest perimeter.

But Robbie's guest appearances were at least something Nathan could rely on. Without fail, every evening between six and eight, he would show up. Nathan was patient. Slowly, he was able to get a little closer to Robbie. And on the seventh month, one calm and starry night, Robbie had allowed Nathan to within seven feet of what the brown furball with big ears obviously considered his space. They shared mutual eye contact for a few priceless moments, only interrupted by the odd noise from the forest, at which times Robbie's big ears would immediately perk up, instinctively aware that any second a predator—fox or coyote, for example—could be nearby, looking for dinner.

The stare-down continued until Nathan dared to breach Robbie's revised seven-foot perimeter. And as soon as it was breached, Robbie made a mad dash for the forest, skidding to an abrupt stop a few feet from the tree-line, turning to acknowledge Nathan, and then disappearing.

When Nathan first met his neighbor, Edward Sole, he proudly announced, "I now have two friends on the Island and they don't give me any grief—Robbie the Rabbit and Mugs the Chipmunk."

To which Ed had tersely replied, "That's because they're not human."

Not human ... not human ... not human ... the thought thrust him into another dream-world dimension.

******

He walked down the street of a Latin American city—where, he knew not. Cars bustled past, pedestrians went about their daily routines; gothic, turn-of-the-century churches loomed ominously, back-dropped by a gray sky. Disoriented, he started asking passers-by where his home was, as if they would have the answers. One long-toothed, grinning black man with an afro poking out in odd directions said: "You want Farrell Road. That's where you'll find your way."

But before Nathan could get clarification, the man wandered off, cackling hysterically at something he found funny. Nathan had no idea what it might be. His purpose now was to get home.

The new landscape was eerily uncomfortable. And nobody would tell him how to get home. Then he remembered. He had company coming. Real friends, not of the furry variety. He had to ready the guest bedrooms, clean the house, scrub the toilet, buy new air-mattresses, maybe even a real bed. A nameless and faceless married couple were coming to spend the weekend with him. He couldn't remember where he might have met them, but yes, they were friends.

He came upon an elderly, hunched-over woman standing at a busy intersection. "I need to find Farrell Road. That's the way home. Can you tell me where it is?"

The woman shook her head, arching her right eyebrow at him as if he had just stepped out of a spaceship from Mars. "Ain't from around these parts," she said. "Have no clue."

She stepped off the curb and began sinking helplessly into a black puddle.

Nathan stepped into the puddle and grabbed her arm. He pulled, but was no match for the force of the black slimy puddle. It sucked her down; flailing and screaming. Then it was only a feeble, long-nailed hand that he held. The puddle had consumed the rest of the woman. Nathan winced, pulled, strained to rescue her, but it was no use. He too began to sink into the hole, along with the disappearing hand.

He grunted and strained and extracted his leg, which had been swallowed to the knee. He still gripped the sinking hand. He extended his other hand to improve purchase, but the black gooey mass swallowed the woman's wrinkled hand and it slipped through his fingers.

Three black bubbles emerged on the puddle's surface, growing into sludge bubbles. One popped and a horrible scream rang out. The other two formed perfectly round, six-inch-diameter balls, and floated up into the gray sky. Nathan watched as one disappeared into the darkness, while the other one popped, emitting a short, shrill, anguished scream.

His hand was smeared with black slime. His right leg was soaked to the knee in the same slime. He got up and began wiping his gooey hand on his unblemished pant leg.

Pedestrians, previously oblivious to his plight, and the plight of the elderly woman, were now surrounding him, maniacal grins contorting multiple monstrous faces.

Terrified, he sprang to his feet and ran across the street. Traffic was halted, waiting for a traffic light to turn green. In the middle of the street, Nathan stopped. A uniformed traffic cop calmly directed traffic, waving a turning lane through with one hand while halting other traffic with the other.

Nathan looked at the street sign: *Farrell Road*.

"Excuse me, sir," he said to the cop, "do you know where Farrell Road is?"

"Farrell Road is two blocks that way," the cop said, pointing to his right.

"This isn't Farrell Road?"

"This is Farrell Road, but not *the* Farrell Road. You want to go that way."

Nathan continued along the bustling streets of the unknown city, panic beginning to knot an empty stomach. Along the way, monstrous faces passed him, smiling wickedly, a few pointing behind.

"It's that way," a grotesquely deformed midget with an oversized head resembling Frankenstein said. "You're going the right way."

The gray sky slowly turning black as he walked, Nathan arrived at a subway station entrance, a sign, *Farrell Subway Station, The End of the Line*, flashing in white neon atop its black rectangular opening.

A few pedestrians ambled toward its entrance, slouching despairingly.

Two black uniformed cops appeared, grabbing him roughly by the shoulders. "You've been sentenced to death," one said. "Come with us."

Nathan struggled as they whisked him down a spiraling staircase, but his efforts were no match for the heavyweights. He was led into a small white room and shackled to a stretcher. The men left, locking the door behind them.

He tried to raise his head, but a tightly bound leather strap around his neck prevented it. He looked around the room, noticing a small table to the right of the stretcher that appeared to contain surgical instruments. *My God, what are they going to do to me?* The room was lit by a single incandescent light bulb swaying on a cord in the middle of the ceiling. There was a black tinted window on a wall across from him. *They're going to watch me die. This is it. The end of the line.*

Open your eyes and it'll all be over, Nathan told himself. *It's a dream. Nothing more.*

He closed and opened his eyes. The same room, same stretcher, same one-way glass window, same surgical table gleaming with polished surgical instruments. Was this the Second Realm, as Ed had foretold?

You're going to die ... painfully ... very soon.

He struggled to escape, strained to move unwilling legs. But he was no match for the strength of steel shackles and leather straps. *You have no friends,* a voice in his head said. *Animals don't count. You're all alone in this world. You live alone and die alone. And now is your time. Face it like a man. Nut up or shut up.*

Faced with this moment of truth, Nathan realized he didn't want to die after all. Maybe the real world was far worse than this nightmare, if it indeed it was a nightmare, but he no longer wanted to willingly succumb to death. The heroic image of the kamikaze airplane fighter precipitously lost its appeal, although the bravery of such an act of valor was unquestionable. No. He wanted to go out fighting, but not commit suicide in the process. If he got out of here, he promised himself, he would curtail the reckless abandon he had demonstrated of late. Fight hard, yes. But fight smart, not stupid. If he landed in the Second Realm with Cadence, that was his destiny. If he wound up struggling in the macabre new world order on Earth with Velvet, well then, that too was his destiny. *Nut up or shut up.*

Before he could continue with the self-taught philosophy lesson, the door opened and in walked a man clad in white surgical garb, complete with surgical mask and cap, and large black-rimmed glasses framing a small face and beady brown eyes.

"Are you ready?" the man asked, picking up a large syringe from the table, eyeing it carefully and squirting a tiny jet of clear liquid from its tip.

"No, I'm not ready," Nathan said, sensing the familiarity of the voice, the posture and black-framed glasses. *Who is that?*

The man set the syringe down, rolled up Nathan's sleeve, swabbed a vein with an alcohol-saturated cotton ball, tied the arm off at the bicep, and tapped lightly on a large protruding vein.

"No," Nathan said with rising panic. "I don't want to die. Not yet. Not like this."

"You die by lethal injection," the man said, picking up the needle and slowly lowering it to the throbbing vein.

Even behind the white surgical mask, Nathan could discern the grin.

And he knew who it was.

A buzzer sounded and he bolted upright in bed, his t-shirt drenched in sweat, heart thumping wildly in his chest.

Doctor Stan Imes's voice, calm and serene: "Wake up, sleeping beauty. I need you in the lab. I think I've found the antidote."

Chapter Nine

Listening to Doctor Imes speak, Velvet wondered if he was telling the truth, and if he was, did she even want the antidote for P-744? She might not like the paranoid side effects, but she sure enjoyed the carnal sessions with Nathan. She had come to view the lust-filled escapist sessions as the only pleasurable thing left to do on the planet, a planet which had become an Orwellian prison. Sure, she loved to read horror novels, watch horror films even, but what horror book or movie could possibly be worse than the one she was living? Reality indeed was not only stranger, but much worse than fiction.

Imes detailed how he planned on reversing the effects of the drug invented to create a super (and subservient) race of soldiers. Watching and listening, Nathan's right eyebrow was arched and his expression shifted between confusion, skepticism and yes—she was sure she saw it from the kamikaze warrior—even fear.

While Mary Anne slept down the hall, Nathan and Velvet sat beside each other in small, ergonomically-designed chairs, listening to Doctor Imes. He stood in front of a large modern green chalk board, a table of test tubes, petri-dishes, microscopes, and other lab equipment spread out in front of him. His tone was almost gleeful. He could have been an enthusiastic chemistry teacher delivering a lesson to eager students. He held a large black wand of sorts in his right hand. As he wrote on the board to illustrate the chemical reactions that were about to occur, the mathematical formulas would automatically illuminate bright yellow, like the modern touch-screen maps used by television weather forecasters and news anchors. He finished explaining the science behind the antidote, turned away from the chalkboard, set down the magic wand, and pointed to a collection of neatly-arranged syringes.

Picking one up, he examined its clear contents proudly: "This should reverse the effects of P-744."

Nathan's right hand gripped his leg, pink knuckles turning white. "You came up with that awful fast."

"On the contrary," Imes said. "I've been working on it for some time. I figured that if things went wrong, we'd need a way out, a way to backtrack from this whole idea of genetically modified soldiers. So I devised a formula for reversing P-744's effects and tested it out on lab monkeys—it seemed to work. Then I destroyed the samples and kept the formula. And I also kept it secret from my superiors ... I can't say I had a lot of trust in them."

Listening to Imes's explanation, Velvet realized that a lot more needed to be explained. Her post-apocalyptic life had been such a dire struggle for survival and sanity, she had never really introspectively looked at the whole picture. North Koreans drop a nuke, following it with a biological weapon, just in case. The mixture creates mutant animals, birds, zombies, and now gigantic flies and spiders are thrown into the mix. What really happened?

The government goes on a mission to genetically engineer civilians into doing their bidding. Why? Why now?

Then there was Nathan's wild mood swings of late and his recent sojourns into the Second Realm. Did it even exist, and was it in some way connected to P-744 and this entire nightmare? "I want to know how it all started," Velvet said. "Where did everything go wrong?"

Imes paused, put down the syringe, and stared at her for a long moment, a curious expression which Velvet thought translated into a reticence to disclose everything.

Nathan continued gripping his leg, looking like he might bolt from his seat at any moment.

"It's a long story," Imes said.

"Give me the abridged version."

"Wouldn't you rather listen to it when you're free from P-744's effects?" Imes said. "So you can process it with a clear mind?"

"No," Velvet said. "I want to know now."

"Likewise," Nathan said. His tone was nervous.

"I want to know exactly what we're up against, so we can make a plan, which I don't think we really have, do we? ... Other than to reverse the effects of your cra"—Velvet bit her tongue—"your invention."

"Okay, okay, I'll tell you what I know."

"Please do," Nathan said.

"The Canadian and American defense departments, in the interest of protecting our countries, commissioned me to make P-744. Once the trials started going well, Commander Stiessman wanted a real-life situation to test it. He wasn't happy with trials, or mock battles with enemies who really couldn't react. So ... they picked the most economically depressed areas of the country and dropped a modified version of a nuclear bomb into very selective target areas. That was followed by a bio-chemical weapon that spawned the zombies,

Neanderthals and mutant animals. It gave them something real to kill—a legitimate enemy."

"Hardly legitimate," Nathan said. "You mean the rest of the country—or the rest of the world—isn't affected?"

"That's where things get a little hazy," Imes said, "because the North Koreans got involved. As far as I know, New Brunswick, Nova Scotia and the Island here were the first targets. But then I heard British Columbia was also bombed, even Saskatchewan and Manitoba. I also obtained information that Stiessman, or maybe Captain Sterling, I'm not sure anymore, sold the technology for P-744 to North Korea. North Korea dropped an attenuated nuke in the Atlantic Ocean. It created the tsunami that destroyed District 101 and Project Nobleman. They did that because they wanted to be first with the perfect warrior. They're a totalitarian regime. They're pulling out all the stops to insure they are first and strongest." Imes sighed, lowering his gaze to the floor. "It seems my invention to create the super soldiers has turned into the perfect invention for the end of the world."

"I'd say," Velvet said. "What about the insects? When we fought here before, I may have seen mutant pigs, mutant birds, but insects? What's happening?"

"I only have a plausible theory on that," Imes said. "Jeffrey Laines, my one-time lab helper who stole my job, was working on a formula—always trying to one-up me, that little shit—that could enhance soldiers even more. Make them stronger, less prone to fatigue, able to live off their own body fat for days at a time without food. But he went a step farther and made them into giants, fifty feet tall, something like that. Anyway, Laines ran some trials with monkeys. They grew strong and tall but something happened to the DNA embedded in the virus they were injected with. They started getting weaker, many getting sick. Most of them died. The ones that didn't we put down. Worried about a government backlash, Stiessman ordered Laines to destroy the formula and all evidence of it. But I saw a vial of it—HL Kane, Laines called it, that had somehow fallen out of a safe disposal bin. There were flies all over it. The spider got the fly and look what happened. Except with the insects, they're clearly getting stronger, and we have no idea how it will affect their life expectancy or whether it will spread to other insects, perhaps even humans."

"I couldn't script this any better if I was a horror writer," Velvet said. The color had drained from her cheeks. "Maybe I'm better off with the P-744. At least I know, I'm sometimes paranoid, sometimes feel like killing Nathan, and sometimes feel like fucking him to death. But I'm definitely stronger and need less sleep than before."

"I think you're missing the point," Imes said.

Velvet stood up. "That's exactly what I'm missing." She gestured to Nathan. "How 'bout a quickie before we go under the needle? I need to get the point. Poke me and then he'll poke you."

******

When Nathan saw Doctor Imes raise the syringe and stare proudly at its contents, he almost pissed his pants with fear and bolted for the door at the same time. But he managed to compose himself, hold his bladder, and listen. He wanted to know what was going on. Now he knew, and he wondered how he could have been so stupid earlier, how he couldn't bring himself to believe it, and Velvet was the one who seemed to know all along.

Maybe it was the amnesia that had created the gap in information processing, Nathan thought. Because it should have been obvious.

He had read about genetic modification and the coming of Big Brother, and knew even then it was closer than many people wanted to believe. Under the guise of doing what's right for the country and keeping its citizens safe, government officials around the world were installing high-tech surveillance systems, a vast network of spy cameras, license plate readers and databases, watching and recording 24/7. Databases interfaced with one another and facial recognition technology was better than ever. Individual profiles were being assembled, stored and studied. Everyone was a potential terrorist and personal liberties, freedoms, and privacy were being eroded and encroached upon under the guise of national security.

There was even talk of the government making it mandatory for everyone to receive implantable microchips. Authorities claimed the microchips were only for the identification and safety of its citizens. Help stamp out terrorism, identity theft, and fraud. Even the banks were coming on board, wanting to make it mandatory for account holders to have microchips embedded in their brains. The government was working to implement legislation making it mandatory to install the microchips to apply for or renew a passport, and government agencies, for so-called security reasons, had already made it mandatory for its employees to have the chips implanted in their brains. Microchip technology had advanced to the point of being able to read your thoughts. Unbeknownst to these microchipped people—maybe they didn't want to believe, or believed the benefits outweighed the dangers—the government was likely monitoring their thoughts 24/7.

Big Brother was watching.

And waiting to act.

Even cops were becoming totalitarian thugs, strip-searching people in public, beating them for no apparent reason, arresting them at random and with insufficient proof.

And now they were much better prepared than ever, Nathan thought. DARPA (the Defense Advanced Research Projects Agency) was working on creating super soldiers, genetically modified trans-humans possessed with super human strength allowing them to outrun Usain Bolt, out-lift Olympic weightlifters, and even regrow limbs. These soldiers wouldn't tire, could go days without food, living off their own body fat. Word had it they could even communicate telepathically with the microchips. Cyborg soldiers, cyborg-law-enforcement officers, with computer technology implanted in their brains, maybe a million nanocomputers, or nanobots, replacing living cells and doing the job much more efficiently, even extending life, messing with creation in such a way as to create immortality.

Real-life superheroes, controlled by psychotic megalomaniacs, fighting their wars for them.

Pre-apocalypse, the world had become a scary place to live in. Paved with good intentions? Maybe. But surely a road to hell.

We were creating our own living nightmare, Nathan thought, his mind drifting back to his own haunting nightmares and to Cheap Trick's *Dream Police*:

> *The dream police, they live inside of my head.*
> *The dream police, they come to me in my bed.*
> *The dream police, they're coming to arrest me, oh no.*
>
> *You know that talk is cheap, and those rumors ain't nice.*
> *And when I fall asleep I don't think I'll survive the night, the night.*
>
> *'Cause they're waiting for me.*
> *They're looking for me.*
> *Ev'ry single night they're driving me insane.*
> *Those men inside my brain.*

He didn't know how long he had wandered. But it was Velvet tugging on his shirtsleeve that snapped him out of it. "Did you hear me?" she asked.

He had heard her. *A poke before a poke, something like that.* And right now, the idea of a piece of ass before an injection sounded just fine. Maybe it was the P-744 creating the urge, but who really cared anymore. He was living in hell, and sex with Velvet was the only reprieve he could think of.

He turned to her. "Sure, I'll make sure you get the point."

Maybe he didn't want an injection anymore, even if it really did mean he would be free of P-744. An injection could be a lethal one, and right now he didn't want to die. Eventually, maybe, but not right now. Not slowly and painfully, as Ed had foretold. *Fuck Edward Sole and the white robe he rode in on.*

Right this minute, other than the desire to preserve his life for just a little longer, there were only two things in the world that he cared about: finding out if the emotion he felt for Velvet Jones was real, and finding out how he could meet Cadence in the Second Realm. And, if the *thing* with Velvet was nothing more than P-744, then he wanted to join Cadence in the Second Realm. That puffy white picket fence on that puffy white cloud, looking down and maybe even laughing at all the self-created misery on Earth.

The nightmare, as horrific as it was, had perhaps also served as a panacea of sorts and given him some clarity of vision. *How the fuck are you going to know if what you feel for Velvet is real if you don't take the injection, fuckbrain? Some clarity of vision you have. As clear as mud.*

Nathan stood up and sat down again, not sure anymore.

"What are you waiting for, cowboy?" Velvet said. "You wanna live forever?"

The P-744 took over. Nathan stood up and followed Velvet to the door. Before closing it, he turned to Imes. "This can wait."

"No it can't," Imes said. "You don't understand."

Chapter Ten

"You don't seem to understand," Commander Rice Sterling told biologist Jeffrey Laines as they sat in the control room of an aircraft carrier in the Atlantic Ocean discussing strategy. Sterling's eyes had narrowed to slits. A large vein in his neck throbbed. "If we can't destroy them, and this gets out, we're going to have a goddamned revolution on our hands. And I won't stand for that. You hear me?"

Laines nodded meekly, not wanting to get in the bad books of his psychotic superior. He knew the cost.

Sterling continued: "You fucked up with HL Kane. You didn't dispose of it properly. Now we've got fucking giant flies, even bigger deadly spiders, wiping out our forces."

"Maybe they'll wipe out our targets," Laines offered.

"I'm not prepared to take that chance," Sterling said, pounding a fist down so hard it spilled coffee on classified documents.

Laines reached for the documents and Sterling grabbed his wrist. "These aren't for your eyes." His steel grip loosened and he released the doctor's wrist.

Laines winced, rubbing the red handprint on his wrist. "I was just trying to he—"

"Never mind," Sterling snapped. "As I said, we only have one available option."

Laines had heard Sterling the first time he had mentioned the word nuke, but it was as if a part of his mind was blocking it out, refusing to believe even Sterling would stoop to such measures. Finally, he said it: "You want to nuke the Island, sir? We still have troops there, some being held hostage by Neanderthals, others trapped in spiderwebs waiting for black widows to dine, still others searching for the targets."

"Haven't you heard?" Sterling said. "When we're at war, that's called collateral damage. Troops are expendable. They knew that when they signed up for this."

Laines thought better of reminding Sterling that the remaining District 101 troops recently dispatched to PEI had not volunteered for the mission. They were under the control of P-744. Laines had also not bothered to tell Sterling the fix he had given those same troops before dispatching them was not permanent. Sterling had given him very little time to tamper with Imes's brainchild and stem the tide of the uncontrollable sexual urges subjects were experiencing, not to mention the uncontrollable violent outbursts they were prone to. So Laines had experimented with various sedatives, finally settling on Lorazepam, or Ativan, a high-potency sedative used in the short-term treatment of anxiety, insomnia, and aggression. As a band-aid solution, the drug had reduced the sexual urges of subjects, as well as inhibited their unprovoked violent outbursts, at least those related to harming each other without cause. Laines knew it was only a matter of time before the Ativan's effects wore off and the troops reverted back to dangerously unpredictable behavior patterns.

But in the short amount of time he had to make the troops battle-ready, it was all he could come up with. He told Sterling he had altered the chemical components of P-744 to produce a "much more desirable effect."

In reality, to do this, he would need at least three months or more of trial-and-error experimentation with lab monkeys.

But with Sterling, Laines had to produce results, and quickly, or else. Sterling's veiled threat after he had put a bullet in Stiessman's head echoed in Laines's mind: *"You stick with me, you'll stay on the bright side of the dirt."*

"Why are you looking so starry-eyed?" Sterling said, snapping Laines from his contemplative pose. "Dispatch the order for a nuclear strike tomorrow at zero-seven-hundred hours."

Laines threw his only card on the table. Problem was, it hadn't worked the last time. "Commander, I urge you to reconsider. As I said, I've been in contact with G-Force team in Montague. They haven't been killed by insects or Neanderthals. They're zeroing in on our targets, on Doctor Imes's underground lab. At dawn tomorrow they're set to go in."

"Why don't we just bomb it again?" Sterling asked.

"Our smaller missiles have been intercepted, sir. Neanderthals and insects, I'm afraid. G-Force is our only hope."

Sterling's eyes narrowed again and Laines tensed, expecting another coffee-spilling fist-pound. But the commander controlled his emotions. He stared at Laines with piercing eyes that Laines now knew were capable of horrible atrocities. After a moment, he said, "I'll give them twelve hours. If they haven't destroyed the targets by then, we launch the nuke. Do I make myself clear?"

"Crystal clear," Laines said. "And thank you."

"You're dismissed," Sterling said, issuing the customary fly-swatting wave.

Before the commander could change his mind, Laines spun around and left, taking meticulous care to close the door gently, knowing only too well the wrath that Sterling could spew at the sound of a door slamming. It was a direct affront to his authority, and he wouldn't stand for that without a severe reprimand.

Taking the elevator down two levels, where his lab and office were located, Laines couldn't help the stiffening in his loins at the thought of her. Only problem was, she wasn't around to service his needs. Marilyn Buxton, former lover to the late Commander Stiessman, was on a P-744-controlled mission with G-Force set to invade Imes's underground lab and research facility at daybreak tomorrow.

Laines always had a thing for Marilyn. So when Commander Stiessman quite literally dropped out of the picture, his urges had gotten the better of him. One night while she was returning to her bunk, Laines had entreated her to come to his room, promising favors and maybe even a way out of the PEI search-and-destroy mission. Of course, Sterling knew twenty-three soldiers were slated for battle and he had counted every one of them that Friday morning as they climbed into waiting choppers. At one time, Laines might have tried to create an illness and fool the commander. But not anymore. His recent experiences with the man's demented psyche served as plenty warning of what he was capable of.

Laines had consummated his relationship with the twenty-five-year-old former stripper the night before the mission. He didn't realize he was in love with her until after she left. As Stiessman had before him, Laines had watched the buxom contortionist buck-naked, humping a bedpost and moaning with pleasure, her ample breasts flopping rhythmically to her gymnast-like gyrations. Under the influence of P-744, Laines knew Marilyn liked it hard, fast, and often, displaying none of the violence blood type A subjects had along with their frequent fornicating tendencies.

Beyond the sex, there was a tenderness about her that Laines found so endearing. A sparkle in her eye, a quick smile, a playful, almost child-like quality that not only reminded Laines of Marilyn Monroe, but touched something deep within his heart that he wanted to protect. A small seed of emotion was taking root. As an only child, Laines had photos of Marilyn Monroe plastered all over his bedroom. One of his childhood dreams was to find a long-term relationship with someone just like her. But his computer-geek appearance and awkward social skills—he was about as outgoing as a bowl of cherries—did little to attract the opposite sex. So he immersed himself in his studies, receiving accolade after accolade for his accomplishments. He vowed to compensate for his social awkwardness by excelling in the creation of bio-chemical weapons and genetic modification drugs. Then people would like, admire, and even love him. And the women, well, they would flock to him like a hungry health-nut to a bowl of cherries. But it hadn't happened that way. HL Kane was a dismal failure, and now the world was a mess. Now, with a future as uncertain as winning at a casino slot machine, there weren't a lot of available women to choose from. So, after Marilyn had popped his cherry, spent most of the night cuddling and talking soothingly to Laines, he didn't see a lot of options. If he wanted her, he would have to go and get her before a nuke destroyed the Island.

Locking the door to his lab, he now realized his heart was beating at what he calculated to be three times its normal rate.

He was giddy with nervous excitement. He flicked on the light, wiped a hand over a sweaty brow, and removed his glasses. He wiped the lenses on his white lab coat and walked over to a white cabinet. Opening a locked drawer with a key, he pulled out a test-tube and grinned as he read the label under bright fluorescent lights:

HL Kane. This ought to do.

Chapter Eleven

Maybe he didn't understand, didn't know what he ought to do, but Nathan had ignored Imes's warning, closed the door, and retreated to Velvet's suite. Now, lying beside her in the double bed, for the first time wrapped in a post-coital cuddle, he thought about the ramifications of volunteering for the antidote.

He stared at the dark ceiling while Velvet slept, or at least appeared to be sleeping. Her arm was wrapped around him, her head nestled on his naked chest. With her finely-honed self-preservation skills, Nathan wouldn't be surprised if she slept with one eye open.

He glanced over at a single flickering red circular light mounted on the wall by the door. An intercom speaker was fastened below it, and Nathan wondered if it was some kind of an emergency alarm. *Isn't it an emergency now?* he thought, as more thoughts tumbled like wet clothes in a dryer. *I need to know if this is real. But what if my nightmare was a premonition? Take the lethal injection and die ... you're going to die ... painfully ... very soon. Then I'll never know. But if the Second Realm is real, I'm sure I'll find out when I get there. Ed will tell me. Ed, Ed, Ed. What to do with Mary Anne? She's here now. Now what? Never mind that for now. Velvet is here, right now, with you—maybe your only chance for a real soulmate in a hostile environment. Say something meaningf—*

"Did you say something?" Velvet asked sleepily.

"No. But maybe I should."

Uncharacteristically, she didn't pull away and retreat inside that inner rock, inner island. She stayed where she was, unmoving.

"What do you want to say?" she asked.

"Is this real?"

"It feels awfully real to me."

"What do you mean? This fucking nightmare or us?"

"I'd appreciate it if you didn't use 'fucking nightmare' and 'us' in the same sentence."

"Sorry."

"Forget it."

"I mean, what we're doing ... the connection we have ... is that all P-744 or is something else happening?"

"You want Black Velvet's answer or Velvet Jones'?"

"I want the truth."

"I wanted to talk to you about this. But ... you've been acting so crazy lately I just didn't know when to bring it up. The timing always seemed to be all wrong."

"I have my faculties now."

"Are you sure?"

"No ... but are we sure about anything anymore?"

"I guess not."

"Tell me what you think?"

After a long pause, she said, "Originally I thought it was just the drug, but now I don't know anymore. And even if it is something real, I don't know if you can trust me ... I don't know if I can trust myself with that emotion. You don't know much about me. Suffice it to say, I've suffered some abuse at the hands of men. I've cocooned myself for years because I couldn't bring myself to fully trust another man in that way. If this is real and I let you in that door, I may throw you out again, slam the door shut and throw away the key. Or worse, throw you right through the door ... I don't know, Nathan. I don't know what to think anymore ... sometimes I don't want to think about anything but how to escape this hellhole, and you're the only person I can trust to help me do that."

"So you do trust me on some level?"

"Some, yes, but not all. Maybe never all."

"Maybe I'm not to be trusted. Maybe I'm not such a great catch. It's not like I'm a model of diplomacy or anything like that. Look at me ... one minute scared to shit, the other I think I'm a fucking kamikaze trying to do something noble. Or I'm having nightmares and talking a bunch of gibberish about the Second Realm ... one second I think I want to die, the next I think I want to live."

Velvet stirred, looked directly into his eyes. "As long as we're both modified, we have no idea what atrocities we're capable of. Trust becomes a daily thing, based on behavior. And that Second Realm stuff. I don't know if it's gibberish. Unless I'm going bat-shit crazy, I *saw* you disappear, then reappear. Maybe there is something to it."

Nathan thought about what she said and supposed she was right.

But he still wanted to know if Velvet was open to the possibility of being with him. "So you don't trust yourself enough to give me a chance?"

"You like me?"

"I think you know that." He lifted his hand and gently stroked Velvet's black, flowing hair. She didn't wince or pull away—hardly moved at all.

"You don't know if what you feel is real," she said. "And I thought you were still hung up on Cadence and blamed me for her death."

"I don't deal with emotions that healthily," Nathan admitted, unable to stop the knot of guilt and shame tightening in his belly. He was starting to comprehend that, Second Realm or not, Cadence was now part of his past—a past, however heart-warming and heart-wrenching, he should put behind him. It had been no more Velvet's fault that Cadence had died than it had been her fault they were living this current horror movie together. "I'm sorry."

"Okay."

They said nothing for a few seconds. Finally, Nathan said, "I guess there's only one thing we can do."

"Take the injection."

"Yes."

"I think you're right. We don't know what we have, really. Don't know if we'll end up like those *subjects* in the so-called deviant wing of District 101. We might try and kill each other again. We've had those thoughts before. Or maybe we'll want to fuck each other to death."

"But what if it's a lethal injection?" Nathan asked, beginning to second-guess his previous words of wisdom.

"I would not run from the holocaust, I would not run from the bomb. I'd welcome the chance to meet my maker, and fly into the sun," Velvet said.

"Lou Reed?"

"Yeah ... I like him."

"Me too, God rest his soul. Great songwriter and poet. You're prepared to die?"

"I don't know, but I thought it sounded cool at the time."

"It did. It was cool. Should we take the injection?"

"I don't trust Imes as far as I can throw him. But we don't have a lot of options. If we die, at least we go out together."

That comment, as flippant as her tone was, Nathan understood, meant an awful lot coming from Velvet. It showed a new level of trust, a sign that over time perhaps she wouldn't throw him out or through the door as she had said. It meant, if their relationship was real, perhaps it could grow, flourish, and mature into a deep bond of love and trust. Maybe then he would be equipped with a few more tools to cope with this nightmarish odyssey instead of being so flip-flop with his emotions and intentions, never mind his skeptical view of his own grip on sanity. It was a constant inner and outer battle, trying to focus his mind to think rationally and reasonably. And a battle, he realized now, that he might have lost a long time ago if it weren't for Velvet.

"You're right," he said. "Let's take it together."

"Okay."

He kissed the top of her head, relieved and grateful for the moral support. Without human companionship, better still a soulmate, the world could be a cold and lonely place. "Thanks."

"For what?"

"For giving me a chance ... a chance to live again."

"Don't thank me yet. We're nowhere near out of this nightmare. The enemy could be close. For all we know, the military is about to drop a bomb on us. Or maybe The Neanderthals are scratching at the door."

"We'll kill them all." There was a silence while Nathan digested the import of his words. As a child, he remembered, he was hyper-sensitive to death, any death. If he stepped on an ant or spider, for example, he would brood about it for hours, mourning the little critter's end. As a teenager, he had once taken a .22 caliber rifle into the forest, aimed at a crow perched on a tree branch about fifty feet away, fired, and killed the bird. The murder, as he viewed it, brought him much grief. Growing up, he never forgot the crow. Every time he saw a crow, he remembered sadly how he had ended the life of one. The painful memory had made him realize he could never become a hunter. But now, wasn't that exactly what he was? A hunter, or at least a soldier. And one who not only held little regard for the lives of others, at least the enemy, but often attached little importance to his own life.

How much he had changed.

Chapter Twelve

A slight change of plan, Imes thought, examining the syringe on the table beside him. At first he didn't believe the Second Realm existed. He wasn't a spiritual man by any stretch. Science, by his definition, ran contrary to many religious claims. And he viewed himself first as a scientist and then a doctor. But in early P-744 trials, a lab monkey had once inexplicably disappeared from its cage, reappearing a full twenty-four hours later, dazed and confused, but nonetheless with a dreamy quality in its eyes, as if it had experienced another, more pleasant world.

At first Imes had dismissed it as nothing more than the attempts of Doctor Jeffery Laines to sabotage his work. He knew the man was gunning for accolades as a measure of his self-worth. But the recent events surrounding Nathan's disappearance and subsequent reappearance led him to question his earlier theories about the possibilities of P-744.

And now, early morning the following day, he had arrived at a new theory—that the Second Realm did exist. And that was where he wanted to be, the only place he could be truly safe from the horrors around him, truly safe from his own psyche. The haunting memories of bloodshed and death created by his own hand were beginning to overwhelm him.

He picked up the syringe, tapping the pulsating vein in his arm. It was a modified version of P-744, and a high dosage. He held it up and squirted some clear liquid into the air. It dribbled down the syringe and onto his white lab coat. It went unnoticed. He wanted a way out, even though he knew that ultimately P-744 was a failure. What he hadn't had a chance to tell Velvet and Nathan was that the violent tendencies and sexual urges subjects experienced only got worse, and not only in subjects with blood type A.

Velvet and Nathan's attraction to one another was purely P-744-induced, Imes believed. Under its ultimately debilitating influence, they would either fuck each other to death, or murder each other in violent rages, rages that would take them far away from anything resembling their own personalities.

Left unchecked, P-744 would drive them into murderous madness.

He had offered them a solution and they had refused. He believed the antidote would give them a fighting chance to reverse P-744's effects and live a "normal" life. But they wouldn't listen. Now, it was time to look after number one. If things went to hell in a hand basket, well, so be it. They couldn't get much worse. And he had antidotes, after all, which he planned on self-administering if things got out of control.

He plunged the needle into the pulsating vein and drained the contents. No more guinea pigs. He was his own guinea pig, finally in charge of his own destiny. The next step was to put himself under general anesthesia, and hope a visit to the Second Realm would be his one and only saving grace. Maybe he hadn't created the perfect warrior. But perhaps inadvertently he had created a way to a more meaningful world; a world where he held a faint hope that all his sins would be forgiven.

Brilliant dancing purple hues—vibrant reds, and bright yellows—appeared, and a surge of adrenaline coursed through his veins. He felt his member instantly harden and simultaneously detected a palpable rage invade his senses.

Then he heard a click. Shit. In his haste to escape this real-world prison, he had forgotten to lock the door.

Mary Anne opened it and peered inside. "What are you doing?"

Through glazed eyes, he gazed at her. *What would she be like in the sack?* He removed the empty syringe from his arm, set it down on the table, and summoned what little control he had of his own faculties. He picked up a full syringe and held it up with an inviting grin. "I'm going to the Second Realm. Care to join me?"

Chapter Thirteen

Nathan wasn't that surprised when he noticed Mary Anne had joined Imes in the lab. After all, she had slept for nearly twenty-four hours and, before she went down, had been told a meeting was to take place there. He didn't think she had any more concept of time than did he. And he wasn't sure how long he had slept after his heart-to-heart with Velvet. He only knew that when he awoke after a long and rare dreamless sleep, she was not in bed.

But she stood beside him now as they stared down at Imes and Mary Anne, both stretched out on small bunks, sleeping peacefully. That did surprise Nathan. Why would she go to sleep beside Imes?

"What happened?" he asked Velvet.

"I don't know," she said.

Nathan approached Imes's lab table and examined its contents; among other things, he saw four empty, unlabeled syringes. He raised an empty syringe to Velvet. "They've taken these."

Velvet rolled up Mary Anne's sleeve, confirming a needle mark. "Taken what, though?"

"Look around," Nathan said, rummaging through cabinets.

Velvet kneeled down and looked under the bed. She raised an empty glass vial and read the label. "Propofol," she said. "What's that?"

"It's an intravenous anesthetic," Nathan said. "Why would he knock them out?"

"I bet the answer lies behind that one," Velvet said, pointing to a locked cabinet behind Mary Anne and Imes.

Nathan found an axe concealed behind a glass case, smashed the glass with his elbow, and extracted it. He was relieved to have an inanimate object on which to focus the rage that was starting to course through his veins, relieved that he didn't have to direct that rage at Velvet. He knew such all-encompassing anger had the potential to propel him to murder. *Kill first, ask questions later.* "Fucking complications," he said angrily, striding over to the locked metal cabinet. "Always fucking complications." He began smashing the metal cabinet. "We decide to take the antidote and now this. Why couldn't"—*thwack*—*thwack*—*thwack*—"anything be easy for a change?"

The cabinet crashed to the floor, its locked door springing open. Pill bottles, test tubes and syringes spilled out. He threw the axe at the wall and it stuck. He knelt down and started rummaging through the spilled contents. He couldn't look Velvet in the face. *Focus the rage. Focus it before it focuses you.*

The found an empty test tube. He read its label aloud: "P-744. They've taken it and then the anesthetic. I'll bet Doctor Imes wants to go to the Second Realm. And it looks like Mary Anne wants to join him."

Velvet stood with her back to the wall, a handgun trained on Nathan.

He looked at her. "What're you doing?"

"Trying to save my life. I know when you get like that. Kill first, ask questions later. Right?"

He fought to control the anger seething up inside him, threatening to spill forth like a long-dormant geyser of oil at any second.

"You're turning red, Nathan. The veins are bulging in your neck."

An alarm wailed suddenly. The sound had a distinct ambulance quality—*waweep-waweep-waweep-waweeeeeep* ... then a monotone female voice: "Level one security breach. Unauthorized entry. For safe evacuation, proceed to level four exit."

Nathan was relieved. Something tangible and deserving to direct his rage at. The timing couldn't be better. "Find the antidote," he said. "Where the fuck is level four exit?"

The monotone female voice replied: "Level four emergency exit located next to research and development laboratory. Please refrain from using profanity on these premises."

Velvet still had the gun trained on him.

"Put that down," Nathan said. "Help me find the antidote and let's go." He fought an urge to grab the axe and smash the speaker into little pieces. Monotone Mona might not like that too much. Besides, she was trying to help them.

Velvet didn't lower the piece, but instead moved cautiously to the door.

The siren wailed.

"Velvet, please. Help me."

She opened the door and was about to disappear, then glanced back at Nathan, now on his hands and knees, picking up test tubes and pill bottles, reading the labels and pitching them across the room. She lowered the gun. "You're not going to kill me?"

"Not as long as I have something to focus the rage on," he snapped. "Come on."

She closed the door and took one cautious step forward.

He held up two tubes of clear liquid. Reading the labels, he said, "Look. P-744 antidote."

The siren stopped wailing.

Monotone Mona: "Elevator containing four unauthorized and armed intruders passing level two. You have ten seconds to proceed to emergency exit or exterminate intruders. Ten ... nine ... eight ..."

Along with assorted other drugs and syringes, Nathan stuffed the antidote test tubes into a medical bag and approached the door. He stopped, looking back at Mary Anne and Imes. Fortunately the hot rage was subsiding. He pointed. "What about them?"

"... Five ... four ... three ..."

"They're under general anesthesia," Velvet said. "What're we going to do?"

"You're right. Let's go."

They closed the door and stepped into the hallway. Velvet stopped, picking up an arsenal of weapons she had leaning against the wall—machine guns, grenades, handguns, even a sword.

"Where did you get that?" Nathan asked.

"While you were sleeping, I've been busy." She offered him a machine gun, a belt of bullets, and a handgun. "I shouldn't trust you with any of this, but what choice do I have?"

Monotone Mona: "... three ... two ... one. You have zero seconds to proceed to emergency exit. Unauthorized intruders disembarking on level three. Option two is to eliminate intruders."

"Come on," Velvet said, picking up her stride. She pointed to the end of the hall leading away from the elevator lobby. "It's the red door."

Nathan stopped, spun around, and fired a burst of bullets down the long, empty hallway.

Velvet spun around, machine gun leveled at Nathan's head. "What're you do—"

A dusty but muscular Neanderthal stepped into the hallway. Velvet fired. A V-pattern of bullets ripped into his chest. "Uggghh," he said, and dropped to the floor, dead.

"Get down," Velvet shouted.

Nathan did.

Velvet pulled the pin on a grenade and tossed it down the hall. It landed, clattered along, and then exploded in the faces of two more incoming Neanderthals.

"Nice shot," Nathan said, getting up and following Velvet, who had broken into something resembling a sprint for the emergency exit.

Waweep-waweep-waweep-waweeeeeeeeep! Waweep-waweep-waweep-waweeeeeeeeep!

Nathan reached the emergency door and stopped, watching Velvet futilely trying to open it.

"Shoot it out," Nathan shouted.

Velvet raised her weapon to fire.

A door not ten feet away clicked open and a voice, eerily familiar to Nathan, spoke: "Not so fast."

Nathan stared down the machine gun barrel at the grizzled face at the end of it. *Karl Mulligan. No. It can't be. I killed him.*

Velvet leveled her firearm at the Neanderthal's head, but Nathan was not so quick to react with a firearm trained at his head.

"Drop your weapon or your boyfriend gets it," Mason Mulligan said as a twisted, evil grin wrought his furry features.

Velvet's finger caressed the trigger.

"I said drop it," Mason said, taking a step closer.

"Not going to happen, scumbag," Velvet said, rolling her eyes dismissively to Nathan, then back to Mason. "What makes you think I give a shit about him?"

"I know you," Nathan said.

"No you don't, Nathan," Mason said. "But you knew my brother, Karl. You killed him."

"He killed Cadence," Nathan said in his defense, realizing as soon as he said it that a Neanderthal was not likely to lend any credibility to his argument, regardless of its merit.

"Do you think I give a shit about Cadence?" Mason said, confirming what Nathan had already surmised. "That slut deserved to die. Just too bad I didn't get to fuck her first."

Nathan flinched, felt the temperature of that not-so-fuzzy warm rage begin to rise. He reached for a handgun and three bullets whizzed past his head, deafeningly close to his right ear. It buzzed with the aftershock like a hive of industrious bees.

For a second, Velvet's attention was diverted to Nathan. His head was tilted over, his hand pressed firmly to his ringing right ear.

It was all the time Mason needed. He stepped forward, grabbed her weapon, and cracked her on the side of her bandaged head with the butt of his gun.

She reeled and fell back into the wall.

Nathan put his head down and charged Mason, slamming him into a wall, an adrenaline-infused rage concoction giving him a strength that belied his slight 166-pound frame. He was hardly an Arnold Schwarzenegger, but in that moment he wouldn't have known or acknowledged it.

Mason crashed into the wall, weapon dislodging and clattering along the floor. Then he bent down, reaching for another weapon.

"Stand back," Velvet shouted.

Nathan, unlike earlier moments when he might well have welcomed a bullet, did not for today's itinerary have one planned, at least not inserted into his body. He doubted the day would go to plan, but it didn't hurt to have one. So he jumped back.

But before Velvet could squeeze off a round, or maybe two for good measure, particularly since she sported another fresh cut—this one on the bridge of her nose—the ceiling above Mason exploded and debris rained everywhere.

And, on a day that had started off full of surprises, still another surprise greeted Nathan, this one not being of the unwelcome variety.

Instinctively firing rounds into the emergency door while shouting, "Let's go, let's go!" to Velvet, Nathan arched his eyebrows as he reached out to grab her and saw a giant white-gloved hand, apparently owned by some giant human, reach into the caved-in ceiling. It located and tightly gripped a shocked and shouting Mason Mulligan and extracted him roughly and rapidly into the newly created hole in the ceiling.

Riddled with bullets, the emergency door sprang open. Nathan held it open for Velvet. "Beauty before age is how the saying goes, I think."

In spite of herself, a smile creased red lips, getting redder by the second from the blood dripping from her nose wound. To the sound of a siren wailing, ceiling crumbling and yet more thumping footfalls, Velvet stepped inside and said, "It's age before beauty, numbskull."

"Whatever," Nathan said. "Let's make like a bird and fuck off."

"Flock off."

"Whatever. Let's get the hell out of here."

Chapter Fourteen

When Velvet and Nathan surfaced through an underground escape tunnel ten minutes later, its steel structure shaking, trembling, and collapsing around them, they emerged into what could be aptly described as hell.

The otherwise gray sky was dotted crimson with explosions, incoming missiles, and swarms of flies attacking military choppers and swallowing mutant birds whole. On the ground, it wasn't a big improvement. Choppers were landing, troops were dispersing, Neanderthals were being shot and killed on sight. It was a take-no-prisoners invasion. Fortunately, and Nathan knew the window of opportunity was rapidly slamming shut, troops were heading toward Imes's underground lab, taking aim at Neanderthals with the same agenda.

There were so many convoluted plots running through this horror story, Nathan couldn't keep track of them all. However, it was easy for him to identify and keep track of the giant man who emerged from the rubble like an angry King Kong on a crushing mission with a tiny blonde woman in the palm of his hand, seemingly oblivious to the carnage around him, whispering sweet nothings into her attentive ear.

Velvet fired a staccato-burst of machine-gun fire at an incoming Neanderthal-driven pick-up truck. It careened right, crashed into a pile of debris, and exploded, punctuating the ashen sky with yet another explosion to add to the cacophony of carnage.

"Look," Nathan said, pointing to the spectacle in astonishment. The giant man's attention turned to the battle at hand. He marched purposefully toward them, crushing vehicles like ants and swatting incoming choppers out of the sky like tiny mosquitoes. He was having a harder time batting away the invading mass of gigantic flies, intent on liquefying him for breakfast. "That's Doctor Jeffery Laines and that test subject, Marilyn Buxton."

"What?" Velvet asked, spinning away from her latest target. She trained the smoking gun barrel at Nathan's head, this time right between the eyes. Then she looked up. "Oh my God. He's coming toward us."

Nathan darted eyes around the battlefield, noticing a pick-up truck lodged against some rubble, engine running, tires spinning in the dirt. The driver window was open. A headless neck with an arm severed above the elbow dangled out. Another arm, this one complete with hand and fingers, hung out. What remained of the man was covered in a yellow spit-like substance evidently regurgitated onto him by a giant fly. The powerful spit-like substance, or vomit as some would prefer to call it, had liquefied him and the fly had consumed a good portion of his remains—probably a morning snack before a full breakfast of humans.

Disgusted, Nathan spit on the ground. "Get that gun barrel off me," he said, pointing to the pick-up. "Over there."

They scrambled to the pick-up. "Don't touch that shit," Nathan said, pointing to the yellow, acid-like substance dripping from the red door. "It'll liquefy you."

Velvet reached a gloved hand into the open window, grabbed the man's torn jean jacket, evidently a symbol for

Neanderthals, and yanked him out. What remained of him slumped to a heap on the ground. Nathan yanked open the door and climbed into the driver seat.

"Sorry for the lack of decorum," he said, pointing to the passenger door. "Hop in."

Velvet climbed in. Closing the door, she said, "I can look after myself. I don't expect anything from men."

"I kind of gathered that," Nathan said, slamming the truck into reverse. It spat dirt, gravel, debris, likely human bones, entrails, flesh, and perhaps even an eye or two. The wheels finally found traction. He peeled away, an impromptu plan forming in his foggy head to drive straight down what remained of Main Street Montague, The Beautiful, turn right on what was once Highway #4, and leave town. A once idyllic and peaceful tourist town had transformed into a chaotic battlefield.

As they drove the ground shook, and buildings, many ruined and flaming from missile strikes, trembled. He made slow progress, and a minute or two later he stopped. His eyes widened in terror and he stared at Velvet, as if she knew exactly what to do and when to do it.

She met his gaze.

There was a ten-foot-tall wall of dancing flames blocking Main Street. Neanderthals squatted behind burned out vehicles, leveling gun barrels at them. Right now, Nathan only wanted one thing: to get into a reasonably safe zone and inject himself and Velvet with the P-744 antidote. It seemed the only thing left to live for.

"What do I do?" he asked, putting the truck in reverse and backing up.

"Turn right," she said, leaning out the window with a ready and willing machine gun.

"Where?" Quickly surveying the scene, it didn't take Nathan long to realize the wall of fiery death extended not only to the street, but also along the sidewalk, perhaps a hundred feet back. He had driven right into a flame-broiled ambush.

Then bullets came, lots of them, smashing the windshield out, ripping into metal and soon flesh.

Velvet opened fire at a parked, smoking vehicle. Three Neanderthals were crouched behind, shooting. She must have hit a gas tank because the vehicle exploded with a whooshing sound. The rising flames caught the transparent wings of an incoming fly, and it instantly transformed into a fireball, buzzing and spinning uncontrollably before the flames engulfed it completely and it dive-bombed into the Montague River. It struck a fishing boat, causing another loud explosion and a whoosh of flames. The explosion caused a domino effect through the water, and other boats caught fire and exploded.

Tingly raw terror snaked through Nathan's intestines and he knew it was time. Time to die. But a gut survivalist instinct prevented him from giving up. He tapped Velvet on the shoulder. She stopped firing and looked at him. "Hang on," he said. "I'm going through it." Nathan's plan added a very literal dimension to the phrase "going down in a ball of flames."

She nodded, tossed a grenade through the windshield, and resumed firing.

He backed up rapidly, thrust the automatic steering wheel shifter into drive, and floored it, white-knuckled, red-faced, and terrified. A lover of campfires and bonfires, he had a new respect for flames, a respect borne of the terrible realization that he would know what it felt like to be barbequed extra crispy. *Here it comes,* he thought. *The painful death that Ed foretold.*

Nathan hit a mound of dirt in front of the fiery wall and the truck flew into the air. Looking down at its trajectory, he realized he hadn't given it enough speed, perhaps hadn't backed up enough before proceeding, hadn't taken the time to work out the irrefutable laws of physics.

Nathan could tell from the vehicle's arc—there was no mistaking it. They were going to crash nose-first into a fiery grave. Whether he had dismissed the notion of a kamikaze warrior or not, the metaphor now seemed appropriate.

But he doubted the tightening in his guts was a true symbol for what the kamikaze must have been like. He doubted the awful fear pumping through his veins was something familiar to them, doubted the panic that was creeping through his consciousness was an emotion they would have felt. He could only think of one thing to say. One hand still gripping the steering wheel, he leaned over to Velvet, pulled her close, kissed her full on the lips, and said, "I love you."

Her eyebrows arched—not in terror, Nathan thought, but in surprise. Her stress-hardened features softened, luscious lips curving upward in a satisfied smile, and she opened her mouth to speak.

No words came.

As the flames licked closer, life-giving and life-taking-away heat growing unbearably intense, Nathan heard a metallic scraping sound coming from the undercarriage. The truck tilted sideways, back and forth, squeaked and squealed, then rose in the air, defying the laws of physics and gravity.

******

When Velvet heard Nathan say the words of endearment, often used so flippantly and without deep import, she almost replied in kind, but then those old trust issues surfaced like an angry serpent, and the words would not come. Besides, on some level, she too was starting to embrace the notion of the Second Realm. She had witnessed Nathan's out-of-body—out-of-mind too, for that matter—experience and realized it was perhaps the last and only chance she would have to be with her late daughter Lisa, the young girl who meant the world to her and was the most important person in her life. She would finally get a chance to tell her how much she really loved her, as if she hadn't said it enough in the past. More importantly, though, she could be with Lisa, abandon this seemingly futile fight, and spend her remaining days in the peace promised by the Second Realm.

Her mind raced back to her last day with her daughter, the day before a nuke sent the world into chaos, death, pandemonium and a daily struggle for survival. Before she died, she wanted to think of Lisa, hoping this thought would propel her to her daughter's side when death placed its final period on a long but colorful story of trauma, pain, suffering and, she hoped in the final analysis, redemption.

Lisa sat at the kitchen table in Velvet's house, eating cereal, eagerly talking about a project on butterflies she was working on for school. The conversation was as fresh in her mind now as it had been then:

"I like butterflies, Mom."

"Me too, sweetie."

"I like how they go from a caterpillar to a butterfly."

"They blossom and bloom, like you, honey."

Lisa smiled. A cornflake had lodged on the right dimple of her cheek, and Velvet lovingly brushed it away.

Lisa continued: "Do you know monarch butterflies fly all the way from the Great Lakes to the Gulf of Mexico and come back to the north in the spring?"

"I didn't know that, angel."

"Yeah, and it's about 2,000 miles."

"A long way to fly."

"But they do it, Mom. They do."

"I believe you. Now finish your breakfast and get ready. Your bus will be here soon."

"Do you know we have over 24,000 species of butterflies?"

"No, sweetie. Wow, you sure know a lot about butterflies."

"I'm learning. I like butterflies. My teacher said when the black bands on the woolly bear caterpillar are really wide, a cold winter is coming. I saw a caterpillar with big black bands the other day. Does that mean a cold winter is coming, Mom?"

The child could have no idea how profound her words would become.

Lisa stood up.

Velvet stood, hugged her daughter, and kissed her three times on the cheek. "I don't know. But I know you're my butterfly. And you're full of warmth. And your mother loves you more than anything on this Earth."

"I love you, too."

"Your bus is here."

Lisa finished her cereal, stood up, fetched a knapsack full of schoolbooks, and went to the door. Opening it, she asked,

"Can we go for a walk in the forest when I get home? I want to see a butterfly."

Velvet nodded, smiling. "Sure, baby. Now get going. The bus won't wait forever."

Those were the last words Velvet ever spoke to Lisa. That was the last time she ever saw her alive.

******

As the pick-up descended into the wall of fire, Velvet closed her eyes, welcoming the fiery grave to "end this world of pain," as Lou Reed had so accurately put it. She absently put a hand in her pocket, and began stroking the tattered but cheerful picture of her daughter when she felt the pick-up miraculously rise into the air.

She opened her eyes wide and looked at Nathan.

He met her gaze with affection and shrugged.

Horrible cries of death, piercing screams, and devastating sounds of buildings being crushed echoed from below as the pick-up reached an altitude of about 200 feet, leveled off, and began a steady forward progress above the devastation.

Velvet looked back and saw it—or more accurately, saw him. The giant face of Jeffery Laines, beady eyes magnified by the signature nerd-glasses, concern etched into skin made coarse and pothole-scarred by magnification. Large bits of yellow plaque and a morsel of meat hung between the cracks of otherwise straight white teeth. Minty breath permeated the truck. At least he didn't suffer from halitosis, which would be unbearably pungent and nasty, given his size.

Marilyn Buxton, focused and battle-ready, clad in military fatigues and armed with a machine gun, was perched in the white lab-coat pocket inside an ink-stained vinyl pen and pencil holder.

A fly attacked and she blasted it out of the sky.

"I'm getting you out of here," Laines said. His baritone voice, carrying a note of panic, perhaps another note of anxiety, boomed over the sounds of war and death, echoing deafeningly inside the small pick-up cab.

He swatted an attacking fly out of the air. It buzzed away in an out-of-control spiral, disappearing into the ominous gray sky.

A few strides later, the painful shrieks became quieter, but were still audible. Distant but distinct cries of the doomed.

Laines knelt down, setting the pick-up on the ground. "Go to the waterfront at Murray River," he said. "There are boats. Get off the Island. At seven tonight, Sterling's going to blow the shit out of it."

There was sadness in his eyes that Velvet thought spoke volumes about a life of doing the wrong things. It almost moved her to tears. Perhaps ultimately motivated by his infatuation with Marilyn, Laines was trying to make amends for his many bad decisions, trying to break out of the prison of peer pressure and social judgment and do the right thing for a change.

And before she could thank him, or say anything for that matter, he spun around and swatted an approaching military chopper out of the sky. It spiraled in the air and crash-landed, exploding on impact. Then he spotted a regrouping swarm of giant black flies advancing and departed, thundering footfalls shaking the ground like an earthquake. The thunderclaps of human hooves grew fainter.

He's trying to redeem his sins, Velvet thought. *A holy purpose?*

Chapter Fifteen

"Holy fuck," Nathan said, attempting to jam the pick-up into drive. He had alertly put it into park during the human air-lift trip out of certain death—didn't want to hit the ground running for fear of destroying the transmission and safe passage away from the searching, investigating, probing hand of death. "A giant man. What next? We try for glorification, and look what we do. Make a fucking mess. Humans are so stupid."

Nathan tugged on the column-shifter some more. It remained stuck in park and wouldn't move.

"Never mind," Velvet said. "He saved us. Just get that thing in drive and let's go."

"Give me a hand."

She leaned over and they reefed on the shifter. Nathan felt comfort and safety in the warmth of Velvet's touch. Finally, jointly, they slammed it into drive. Bald tires spun for a second, then gripped a pock-marked asphalt surface, and the vehicle lurched forward—forward and away from one disaster and, for all they knew, into another one of equal or greater magnitude and destruction.

"Where to?" Velvet asked.

"I guess where Laines said. To Murray River."

"You don't think he's setting us up?"

"Would he have rescued us only to set us up? He could have killed us then."

Velvet wiped the bridge of her nose, which now was crusted with coagulated blood, and considered this. "I suppose you're right. What about Imes and Mary Anne?"

"Not much we can do for them, if they're not already dead," Nathan said. "Maybe Laines will rescue them. He seems to have become the new larger-than-life superhero."

"The HL Kane," Velvet said. "Like Imes said."

Nathan nodded. "But Marilyn Buxton was an unexpected twist. Love will do strange things to you, I guess."

Velvet nodded, her battle-weary features softening for a second before she donned the warrior face once more. "You got the antidote?"

Nathan nodded, pointing to the back seat.

She leaned over and retrieved Imes's medical bag, folding a protective arm over it. "When are we going to take it?"

Nathan had originally planned on driving to his house, his acreage, but after a while thought better of it. Surely Neanderthals or the military would be waiting for them there, if the house wasn't already ransacked and destroyed. Too obvious. "Soon. I know an abandoned cabin off the highway, about five minutes from Murray River. We'll inject it there, then stay until we see what the side effects might be like before going to Murray River. It's close."

"Laines said the Island's toast at seven tonight. What time is it?"

"Almost noon," Nathan said, pointing to a digital dashboard clock radio.

"Do you think it's accurate?"

"It's not nightfall, we know that. The sky would be a lot darker."

Through the smashed windshield, Nathan peered up at the gray sky. The sun was barely visible through human-produced clouds of pollution and contamination. A black funnel cloud circled ominously. The wind was intensifying. It was getting colder.

They drove under the cloud, both craning their necks to peer inside. Blackness. "There's no light at the end of the tunnel," Nathan said. "No pun intended."

"Let's hope there's a light at the end of our tunnel," Velvet said.

"Is that what you want?"

Velvet was silent for a long time, contemplating the meaning of the question.

When she finally spoke, it wasn't what Nathan expected from the usually decisive Velvet Jones.

"I don't know."

Chapter Sixteen

Deep in what was once thick forest, gray, twisted trunks and decaying overhanging branches surrounded them like grieving tombstones in a tree cemetery. Nathan didn't know if the forest would ever come back. But he did notice some faint patches of green in the otherwise bleak landscape. He knew Mother Nature had an amazing capacity to renew and rebuild herself.

Hiking through his forest one day, he had come across an old dumpsite just off a small hiking trail; a circle of debris, brown rust jutting up from the ground at odd and unnatural angles against a beautiful backdrop of fall foliage: vibrant reds, golden yellows, bright yellows, and dark greens, the colorful and artist-inspiring fall colors that PEI has become famous for.

Surveying the pile of garbage, probably over fifty years old, he couldn't help noticing patches of green jutting out, little trees struggling but growing against overwhelming odds. A pine tree, for example, stood straight and proud, perhaps ten feet tall, smack in the middle of the pile of rusting metal, broken glass, and chemical contaminants. It had taken root in a small hole in a metal paint can. Mother Nature, against overwhelming odds, had found a way out.

******

They arrived.

Sitting cross-legged in the small and uninsulated cabin, the medical bag on the ground beside them, Nathan stared at the surrounding green patches. It wasn't missed on him that he was probably looking at a miracle of sorts. But other, darker thoughts—black clouds of doom—also swirled in his mind. *We destroy and Mother Nature rebuilds. But at what cost?*

Driving down the meandering road earlier, two decaying trees—a warning?—had creaked, groaned, and come crashing to the ground, one landing in the pick-up's path, another a few feet behind. *Don't fuck with Mother Nature.* Angry trees, vying for vengeance.

It had taken Nathan and Velvet about thirty minutes to clear the splintered chunks of maple blocking their path. Initially resistant to the idea, thinking maybe the logs had more fight left, that the initial assault was just a precursor to perhaps some final death blow planned for the near future, Nathan had finally acquiesced, and they had thrown the pieces in the back of the pick-up. Another less superstitious and more rational part of him knew the nights could get awfully cold since man had destroyed the natural climate. Firewood might be welcome later if the pick-up wouldn't start. At least that way he could die sitting around a campfire, with any luck holding hands or hugging the only friend he had left in the whole world.

He loved campfires. And he was pretty sure he loved Velvet.

He rubbed his hands together, blowing hot air into them. His breath condensed rapidly, forming cloud vapor that floated lazily into the air and slowly dissipated. He was getting cold. The wind was intensifying, the temperature dropping. Maybe they would need that campfire sooner than later.

Velvet had been quiet for a while. Her arms were folded across her chest, her green eyes focused intently on the medical bag. Her body language at the very least suggested she wasn't interested in conversation at the moment. At the most, it said,

Keep your distance, or in Velvet-speak, "Stay the fuck away from me and shut up." And for the last fifteen or so minutes, Nathan had honored the nonverbal cues, taken a cup of shut the fuck up, as Ed might have once said before being deified. But the sporadic silence, punctuated eerily by the odd distant explosion, faint buzzing of giant flies, and trees, brushed by the winds, hissing, moaning and groaning, was starting to wreak havoc on his mind.

And after the earlier near-uncontrollable rage, he had no idea when the rage might return. He might decide to grab Velvet roughly by the throat and strangle the life out of her. On the flip side, he had no idea when she would decide to serve up the same gratuitous violence against him.

He knew one thing. The rage was beginning to terrify him. And lately it not only seemed to be getting stronger and more frequent, but also more powerful and forceful than the sexual urges brought on by the genetic manipulation. He didn't know if soon the rage would overpower the "love" aspect of the drug and send him careening helplessly into a murderous tantrum. Maybe he would even hunt down an operating chainsaw and start taking his rage out on the decaying forest.

His mind spun into the forest again, and he thought perhaps the trees were readying for one final assault, one final death blow ... *slowly and painfully* ... Their moans, groans, and hissing certainly spoke of anger and unalloyed rage.

He glanced at Velvet quickly, rubbed his hands together again and blew more condensing breath into them. He looked at the pick-up parked in front of the cabin. Broken tree limbs poked out of its truck bed, bigger severed body parts resting below them. The forest had every reason to attack, Nathan thought. They had kidnapped and were planning to burn the severed remains of one of their own, maybe a brother, mother, or distant cousin. But the fallen maple was already dead. Weren't they giving it a proper funeral, a cremation of sorts?

The wind hissed. A tree creaked, groaned and cracked—long and loud—and smashed into the forest floor a few feet behind the pick-up, splintering into pieces and rocketing in different directions, as if confirming Nathan's dark reverie.

Velvet grabbed her assault rifle, jumped up, and aimed it at the partially open cabin door. Realizing it was a fallen tree, she lowered the weapon and turned to Nathan. "Do you want to start a fire before we shoot up? I'm getting cold."

After his dark contemplation, Nathan didn't know what to think of the plan. But fingers stiffening from cold, condensing breath, and the thought that at least if he was building a fire it would give him something to focus on, a productive and therapeutic cause that would perhaps help alleviate some of the dark thoughts pervading his mind, finally decided it. "Good idea. I think you read my mind."

"I doubt that," Velvet said, producing a black Bic lighter from her pants pocket and going outside. "Only you know what goes on inside that complicated psyche of yours."

Nathan accompanied her outside. In the middle of the clearing, as far away from the overhanging branches as possible, they first gathered small, dry twigs and placed them in a pile. Velvet retrieved a *Playboy* magazine from the pick-up and began tearing it into pieces, crumpling them and positioning them below the mass of kindling. "I don't even know sometimes," Nathan said.

A few seconds passed. Velvet looked at him in bewilderment. "What are you talking about?"

"I find a lot of dark thoughts invading my mind lately."

"Try and push them away," Velvet said, lighting the crumpled mass of nude pictures and articles. "I think maybe it triggers your rage. And I'm getting a little nervous about it."

"So am I," Nathan said, adding some small branches to the fire. It wouldn't be long before they could move to the bigger severed limbs, hopefully without deadly repercussions. They had enough to worry about without being smashed to pieces by a righteously angry forest.

A few minutes later, sitting together on a large log they had rolled close to the rising flames, Nathan watched black smoke and was reminded of cigarettes. He had almost forgotten he was a smoker. He felt around in his pockets, realizing he didn't have any. They wouldn't have survived the water-soaked journey that finally brought him here.

"What're you looking for?" Velvet asked, a bit too curiously.

"Smokes. With all the other shit, I forgot I even had that vice."

"Me too," Velvet said, producing a pack of smokes from a pocket of her military fatigues.

"Where did you get those?"

"My room in Imes's lab. Must have been a smoker in the crowd. Don't think they're gonna miss them, if they're even alive."

They lit up, smoked and stared at the fire contemplatively for a few minutes. For the moment, the explosions and buzzing, and even the wind, had died down. The sky had darkened considerably, turning a black-red. High in the sky, fast moving black clouds announced the coming of a different weather mass—a storm, perhaps. Beside the fire it was warm, cozy, and windless. *A moment of calm before we die*, Nathan thought.

As if reading his mind, Velvet asked, "What time is it?"

He checked the truck's clock radio. 3:46 pm. He relayed the time to Velvet, adding, "If it's accurate, we have a few more hours to get off the Island." He wondered why they seemed so calm about the impending doom; didn't seem in any hurry to leave their posts. But it wasn't rocket science, even though the missile coming their way in a short time had a lot to do with that subject. They had been through so much trauma lately, so many near-death experiences, they had developed some sort of a resistance to disaster. They'd built up an immunity of sorts, whereby their bodies and minds knew exactly what kind of conditions and mindsets were necessary for survival. Nathan had no idea if any of it was true, but at least it was a working, plausible theory, even though it had not been put through rigorous testing or a double-blind study. So he clung to it, finding the notion confidence-building. The ability to relax in the face of certain disaster. Now that was a trait people would give their eye-teeth for. But if this bravado was brought on by the P-744, wouldn't it disappear as soon as the antidote was delivered, if the antidote even worked?

Possibly, Nathan thought, but doubtful, considering all they had been through. No. They were different people now, people who knew how to face danger head-on and come out the other side tougher and with a will to survive. Slowly, he was becoming resistant to, and less surprised or horrified by, bloodshed and chaos; more willing to pick up the pieces after an insane and disconnected introspection; often questioning, downplaying and ignoring the pervasive will to live.

Regardless of the insane nightmares, near-uncontrollable rage, sudden but temporary disregard for his own life, something was taking place inside Nathan quite apart from any human machinations or inventions. He was growing a suit of armor, a full metal jacket, and one small part of him—in spite of the shit-storm he was in, even though only moments ago was frightened the forest would swallow him whole—felt a tingle of pride at the transformation.

Returning from the truck, throwing another much larger log onto an already blazing fire—*go to hell, attacking forest*—all of these thoughts passed through his mind at jet-speed.

He sat down and looked at Velvet. She was gazing into the fire, lost in thought. Slowly her gaze met his, directly.

And then, perhaps the most important thought, the one that would prove or disprove whether this lethal combination of bravado, psychosis, apathy, and rage was nothing more than a megalomaniac-created living nightmare, the one that would prove or disprove whether his love for Velvet was real or part of that failed attempt at perfecting humanity, formed, gelled and cemented itself in his mind. "It's time," he said, enjoying the contemplative glint of Velvet's beautiful green eyes.

He didn't have to explain anything.

She nodded as perfunctorily as a proficient nurse aiding a renowned surgeon at an operating table who just asked her to pass the scalpel, please.

"Yes," she agreed. "I'll get the needles."

Chapter Seventeen

Maybe it was his late father's constant needling, constant reminders that "everything in your life depends on how much control you have," that had led Commander Rice Sterling to this very moment, he thought, sitting in his command office. He was staring deliriously at the blinking red button that controlled the nuke about to annihilate PEI. But, if he had to get really introspective, and he wasn't the type of man to do that, he just wasn't sure anymore. Somewhere along this journey to the top of the control ladder, the reasons had become lost, lost in the pure, delicious enjoyment of pursuing and obtaining power and influence over others. Lost in the adrenaline-surging glee he felt watching others cow-tow to his orders and reprimands. Lost in the euphoric and "natural high" of being the one in power, the man at the top of the power totem pole, the one in control. And lost, too, in the indescribable feeling of satisfaction he felt in the sure knowledge that his late mother, who had inserted a shotgun into her mouth and blown her life to smithereens, had indeed been wrong. Perhaps she didn't realize the cruel irony of her situation, writing a suicide note stating, "Control is an illusion," then picking up the gun, taking control of her fate, ending her long-suffering and miserable existence.

Control was no illusion, after all. It was real and he had it.

And, if things went to plan, he would soon have more of it, he realized, a hand hovering over the flashing button, satisfied with his shallow yet satisfying analysis of control. His hand descended closer to the button. Perhaps now was the time to put what remained of the tiny Island population out of its misery. He brought the hand closer still and it quivered, not with nervousness, but with the anticipation of the adrenaline-surged, euphoric high he was about to enjoy. He had heard his mother Anise once say "Never underestimate the highs of a good conversation." He thought the pearl of wisdom should be reconstructed: *Never underestimate the highs of a good position of control.*

For a moment, Sterling got lost in the anticipation of the giddy glee he would soon experience, and his fingers brushed against the polished flashing red glass of the button. It was warm to the touch and he felt a hot flush of excitement paint his cheeks red. Then he stopped and came to his senses, if he ever had any. No. Now was not the time. A time for everything. And everything had its time. Like some jittery heroin-addicted junkie in desperation for that next fix, he had almost pulled the pin—or pressed the button—too early.

Now was not the time. Soon, but not now.

He steadied his perspiring hand, withdrew it from the button and placed it on his desk. He checked the time: 5:56 pm. Jeffery Laines had been ordered to bring back Imes alive. Sterling had ordered Laines and his team to "shoot Velvet and Nathan on sight," but he wanted Imes alive. Imes, through his neglect and misdiagnosis, had essentially murdered Sterling's wife. Sterling had decided, after Imes's unanticipated escape, that a slow and brutal torture would be a more fitting end for the nutcase.

So he would wait. Wait until he had Imes firmly in his clutches and yes, suffering, and then he would press the button and destroy PEI. He didn't really care anymore whether the mission to PEI was a success or not. On some distant and unreachable level, he realized he was acting on emotion and not logic, something his late father Bryce had told him never to do—"Don't let frivolous emotion cloud your judgment"—but it was too late. The addiction to control had become much too powerful. It was an angry, hungry demon that must be fed constantly.

And part of that feeding ritual also had to do with the elimination of Jeffery Laines, who had not only begun to ask too many pointed questions about Sterling's ambitions, but had recently gone off the radar during the mission to PEI, after convincing Sterling that he wanted to join the G-Force team, monitor their activities, aid them in the mission. Sterling hadn't heard from Laines in over three hours—hadn't heard from any of the troops. Of course, some were dead or dying. And initially he thought Laines had met an early and untimely demise. But when he had powered up a GPS tracker he had secretly embedded in Laines's shirt collar ("Always have a back-up plan," his father had warned) and saw an inordinately large radar blip first moving toward the underground laboratory and then, with rapid and unexplainable strides, moving away from it. Repeated attempts to contact Laines had been met with static white snow. For all Laines knew, the only GPS tracker was imbedded in the walkie-talkie he carried. It looked like he had his own agenda, had ditched the walkie-talkie, and was executing it with no regard for orders from the top. Insubordination. Something that could not, would not, be tolerated. No. Laines had to die. That was the only answer.

But then, as if disproving his theory, a wall speaker squawked, followed by snowy static. When it cleared, Jeffery Laines spoke: "Come in, Black Owl. This is White Owl. Come in ..."

Sterling dismissed the formalities and code names. "What are you doing out there?"

So did Laines. "Most of G-force is dead. But I have Imes—he's alive—and another soldier. We'll be landing in five minutes."

"Did you accomplish the rest of the mission?"

"We did, sir."

"Nathan and Velvet?"

"Dead, sir."

"Good. I want you in my office for a briefing as soon as you arrive. You got that?"

"Roger that, sir. I'll be there."

Chapter Eighteen

As he lay in a cot, bundled up tightly in blankets, Nathan didn't know if he was here or there. Here, being actually in the cabin, next to Velvet, or there, being somewhere between Earth and the Second Realm. After they had injected themselves, a consuming fatigue had settled in. They had abandoned the fire, retreated inside to experience the effects of the injections that, for better or worse, were about to change the course of their lives irrevocably.

Nathan wondered if Velvet was seeing the same images he was. He wondered if it was truly the antidote they had injected, or some other weird mind-and-personality-altering substance created by Imes. Suspended in some strange dark midway point between Earth below and some beckoning, warm, suffused yellow light above, seemingly drawing him higher, Nathan tried to make sense of the vision, dream, transformation, whatever it was.

Looking down through a black swirling funnel cloud—literally tunnel vision, he thought—he could see the cabin getting smaller, a tiny black square in a gray landscape, punctuated by orange-red exploding dots; almost a demonic, perverted version of twinkling stars against the black curtain of night. The fire, one time looming large with intense heat, was now only an orange flickering dot among this constellation of explosions, a tiny stream of gray smoke twirling up into the dark sky.

Slowly drifting up in a prostrate position, he tried to right his extremities, without really knowing why he would want to be in a standing or walking position in a world in which he floated uncontrollably. Maybe it was man's need to impose order and structure on an unstructured existence, some inner genetic calling to try and make sense of it all. He didn't know, but he tried all the same. And failed.

He looked up at the warming, welcoming, yellow beacon of hope. The small circle of light grew as he neared, brilliant hues of bright colors now dancing around it: bright reds, dazzling purples, intoxicating shades of green, azure blue, and other colors, fanning out and forming neat little circles of light around the growing yellow circle.

He somehow felt he was here, but also there, in the cabin with Velvet. And it was very different from previous gravity-defying journeys. There was no fear, no anxiousness, no nervous tension or cold, haunting terror.

Somehow, it seemed just as it should be. His perspective flashed for an instant back to the cabin. He was on the cot, staring up at the ceiling. Beside him lay Velvet, doing the same thing.

"Velvet," he said. "Are you seeing this?"

Silence.

Suddenly he was in the dark funnel cloud again, suspended and floating toward the kaleidoscope of brilliant colors. And Velvet was beside him. They twirled ever so slightly as they floated up.

"The colors," she said. "Amazing."

"Is this real?" he asked.

She smiled, a smile so warm, wonderful, and worry-free; as if everything was right, just as it should be. "It feels real. If it feels real, it probably is."

"But we're in the cabin," Nathan said. "We were in the cabin."

The kaleidoscope of colors fanned out, enveloping them, suffusing them with its satisfying warmth. "Not anymore. We're on the highway to heaven."

Nathan smiled. He didn't remember a time when he felt so utterly happy. He reached a hand out, wanting to touch Velvet, feel her smooth skin, share this precious moment with her. It's not the same unless you share it with someone. Nothing's the same unless you share it with someone. The enjoyment, true enjoyment, comes from sharing happiness, spreading it around. Share the love. But then a dark thought, like a tiny lightning bolt, seared through his brain and exploded, interrupting this flow of trance-like, meditative joy. He pulled his hand away from Velvet. *Cadence. Where's Cadence?*

Velvet's expression transformed into amazement, astonishment; no, she was actually awe-struck, Nathan thought. She pointed at a face materializing in the swirling rainbow of colors, at first hazy and unclear, but then clear and unmistakable. Her daughter Lisa, with a bright smile and azure green eyes, was looking intently and lovingly at her mother.

And, *no it can't be,* Nathan thought. He rubbed his eyes, blinked, and refocused on the image. Blonde-haired, blue-eyed Cadence, now holding Lisa's happy hand, smiling warmly down at them.

"We're okay," Cadence said. "Fulfill your mission. Both of you. You're running out of time. Fulfill your mission in war. Fulfill your mission in love."

And, before either of them could utter a single word, the happy images of the woman who had meant the world to

Nathan and the girl who had meant the world to Velvet vanished in a heartbeat.

******

"Cadence, Cadence ... come back. Cadence ... I love—"

"—Lisa, honey ... your mother's coming for you ... Lisa wait, Lisa don't go ... don't gooo ... don't goooo—"

"—Velvet, Velvet, we have to go—"

"—I'm coming, baby, I'm coming for you ... Lisa ... Lisa, talk to me ... please, please ... say some—"

Nathan knelt down beside Velvet's cot now, gripping her shoulders, shaking her. He didn't know what time it was, but it was late, what was left of the twilight was rapidly being snatched away by the black cloak of nightfall. If they didn't leave soon, they would be blown to shit by the nuclear bomb. And Nathan didn't want to leave Earth anymore, even though it was still a Godforsaken planet. He had been searching for answers, and one had come and pounded a truth into the mourning, grieving, and perhaps guilty neighborhood of his heart. Cadence was okay. It was time to put the past in the past, time to try and put an end to this man-made devastation, time to find out if he was really cured from the debilitating but sometimes euphoric effects of P-744. Time to put Doctor Imes's genius to the test.

Eyes wide open, worry etched in her brow, Velvet squirmed in his grasp, staring at the wooden ceiling of the small cabin. There was a faraway look in her eyes, as if somewhere in the recesses of her mind she was still floating up in the funnel cloud, floating toward Lisa, perhaps the one and only person who she trusted completely.

"Velvet," Nathan said. "Wake up. We have to go." As he said it, he wondered if his words, his interruption of her antidote-induced experience in the afterlife, would have some permanent, debilitating effect on her psyche, maybe even kill her. But what choice did he have?

Her mesmerized eyes focused and she stopped calling out for her daughter. She met Nathan's concerned expression directly. Her body relaxed and he loosened his grip. The joyful, carefree smile did not return to her face. But at least a Velvet expression emerged, one that told him she was in control of her faculties again, ready to fight and survive.

Nathan released Velvet and slumped on the floor beside her cot; the experience had drained his reserves.

She sat up in bed. "How do you feel?" She asked the question as perfunctorily as if she hadn't been thrashing around a few seconds ago, crying out pleadingly for the company of her deceased daughter Lisa. She asked the question as if she had just woken from a dreamless and rest-filled sleep.

Nathan didn't initially know how to answer. On some level felt relieved, like the giant anchor of guilt and mourning had been mercifully lifted from his shoulders, that somehow that giant steel wrecking ball of regret that had been tearing his guts to mush had been extracted, its operators taking a permanent leave of absence. But seeds of doubt started to creep back in. Maybe they were just taking a union-contract-specified fifteen-minute coffee break and would return with renewed vigor and malicious intent, raise the wrecking ball and smash through that wall of shame like it was a thin pane of glass, send flying jagged scimitars shooting through the air with malicious intentions. But he quashed the seeds of doubt, would not give them a fertile garden in which to germinate, take root and spread their confidence-sucking, poisonous weeds.

There was something else, more powerful, certainly more noteworthy. Although his head ached dully—a steady, almost rhythmic throb, a ball-peen hammer tapping on his brain—he couldn't feel the rage, rage that previously boiled just below the surface of rational thought. Rage that had a mind of its own and would explode like an angry geyser at the least provocation, explode at certain triggers he could never actually explain or remember. But now the boiling, bubbling geyser of rage was a calm and serene lake, a glass-like body of water that would mirror the clouds and surrounding landscape as flawlessly as only Mother Nature could.

And something else. Although his head throbbed, as he stared at Velvet, meeting her gaze, his member did not. He didn't know enough about P-744 to remember its cycles. The euphoric sexual highs and rage-filled lows seemed almost to wipe the memory clean afterwards. So, maybe the sex cycle had yet to begin—for that matter, maybe the rage cycle had yet to begin. But he didn't think so. Looking at Velvet, he realized he did like her. But was it—could it be—something stronger?

He didn't have an answer.

Velvet waited patiently, looking at Nathan like he was an idiot savant solving a complicated math problem in his head. "Well?" she asked. "How do you feel?"

"I have a headache."

She rubbed her temple and frowned slightly. "Me too."

"But I feel better. Different. You?"

She wiped away a tear. "Yes, better ... different. I know I freaked out a bit there, but it was a big relief, a huge relief, knowing that Lisa is okay. I guess I just wanted more. You saw her, right?"

"Yes. You saw Cadence?"

"Yes."

"They're happy," Nathan said.

"Yes."

Outside in the darkness, the wind whipped. It snapped a large branch off a decaying tree, sending it crashing to the ground ten feet in front of the pick-up, splintering everywhere, one broken limb thumping onto the hood with a dull clang. It brought Nathan back to their current reality, and self-preservation. "Velvet, we don't have time for reflection. We've got to get off the Island. Unless you want to die."

"Not right now."

Chapter Nineteen

"It's now or never," Jeffery Laines told Marilyn Buxton as they sat in his laboratory on the aircraft carrier. "You have to kill him." He had briefed her on the plan. But it didn't appear much of it had sunk in, or perhaps she didn't care to listen.

Marilyn, clad in a diaphanous white negligee that left little of her voluptuous figure to the imagination, twirled her finger around a pencil. She arched, staring at the pill bottle as if it would grow fangs and bite her throat any second. "I can't do that. I can't kill someone."

Laines sighed. He didn't have a good feeling about the upcoming briefing with Sterling, and he was late already. He checked his watch. 6:18 pm. In forty-two minutes, he was pretty sure Sterling was going to level PEI even though Laines had captured Imes and lied about the fate of Velvet and Nathan. Maybe they were dead by now, but he had no proof of that. In a moment of weakness and overpowering guilt, he had done the right thing. Rescued them and given them another fighting chance at survival. Whether they still had the intestinal fortitude for it, well, that was their problem now.

Imes hadn't been so lucky. Laines still harbored resentment, even hatred, for Doctor Imes. He could not bring himself to release him when he found him in a deep coma, alongside an unidentified woman, in an underground laboratory. So he'd captured Imes, and was about to take the comatose woman along for the ride, but he realized her heart had stopped. Whatever drug they had taken had been too strong for her elderly heart. She had evidently died of a heart attack.

But unconscious Imes was securely incarcerated, handcuffed to a bedpost in a white-padded cell right next door to Laines. Imes was in line for an interrogation from Sterling, an interrogation Laines suspected—knew, really—would be full of bloodshed, cruelty, pain, and suffering.

Torture.

Thoroughly unconvinced about his own longevity, at least among the living, he knew it was only a matter of time before Sterling personally killed him or had one of his underlings carry out the task fearfully but dutifully. So Laines had devised a plan to end Sterling's opportunistic, ruthless rise to the top of the control ladder. He had seen Sterling ogle Marilyn in the past, had turned green with jealously on a few occasions even, and now realized it was his only chance to put the control freak out of his misery. No, you couldn't call it misery, could you? Sterling glorified himself, viewed himself as somewhat of a god. He enjoyed, relished in, and thrived on this control. Laines knew he wouldn't stop until most, if not all of humanity, was dead or firmly under his powerful thumb—a thumb that at any minute might be hovering over the pulse of a bomb. So Marilyn was his only chance. Seduce the sicko, spike his drink with a cyanide pill, and end once and for all his maniacal, meteoric rise to the top of the food chain. Cleaning his eyeglasses on his lab coat, as he often did when devising a plan or working out some complicated formula, Laines believed that this plan was also his only chance—if indeed such a thing as heaven really existed—at redemption. Everything he had done in his life, all the stupid inventions, the phony and pretentious peer accolades and recognition, had led to this very point. Maybe he did have his own agenda, he knew that was part of it, but in his conflicted, HL Kane-infected mind, he also hoped his actions were motivated by some shred of decency, some shred of sympathy—and yes, even love for humanity.

He finished wiping his glasses and put them on. They magnified his black, beady eyes to almost twice their normal size. He finally looked at Marilyn. God, she was beautiful. Stunning, really, a dream come true. And he thought her sex appeal and playful personality would work its magic on Sterling. But he would have to be very delicate. He would have to use what means he could to motivate her to action. "Honey, I rescued you, don't forget. And I have Imes's antidote for P-744. You want to be normal, don't you?"

"Of course I want to be normal," she said, fluttering those deep blue Marilyn Monroe eyes. Her hand moved across the table and caressed Laines's fingers.

In spite of himself, Laines slowly withdrew the hand. "You get this done, I'll make you normal."

"I am normal."

Time was running out. "Marilyn ... you've killed people."

Her eyes darkened, a sadness washing over her pretty face. "I have?"

Laines knew he would have to soften the blow if he was going to get her to cooperate. "Not you, but a modified version of you."

"I couldn't kill anyone."

"I know you couldn't, baby." Laines wished he could activate the P-744-induced violence somehow, but lately the drug's effects came and went unchecked and uncontrolled by man's chemical, or any other verbal intervention. Leaving PEI, he had spoken the violence-deactivation command to no avail (having to physically rescue Marilyn from the heat of battle) to a handful of troops pinned down by Neanderthals, in a firefight for their lives. The troops stopped firing briefly, stared at him blankly for a few seconds, and resumed their attack with seemingly more deadly intent and rage than before. As he floated above the carnage in an escaping chopper, reduced to his normal size after the HL Kane effects wore off, he watched with horror as many soldiers were shot down and killed. Killed in a battle in a war for a cause he no longer understood. And they certainly didn't.

"But, please, for the sake of humanity, do it this once," he pleaded.

Marilyn was petulant and insistent. "Give me the antidote first. Then I'll do it."

A loudspeaker on the wall squawked. It was Sterling's angry voice. "Doctor Jeffery Laines. Where the hell are you?"

"I'm on my way." He knew if he didn't move immediately, troops would be coming to take him forcefully. He suspected troops were probably on the way right now to incarcerate Marilyn, take her out of commission, and eliminate any threat she might pose. Although Laines had turned off what closed-circuit TVs he knew existed in his quarters, he suspected Sterling had a few bugs planted in his combination apartment suite-research and development laboratory. Sterling was methodical in his madness, unwilling to leave anything to chance.

Marilyn pouted.

Laines walked to the door. Before closing it, he pointed to a white cabinet on the wall. "The antidote—P-744 A—is in there. Please, take it and save me. Save everyone from this madness."

She smiled wanly, examining a broken fingernail with a frown. "I'll think about it."

Chapter Twenty

Closing the door to Sterling's command room, Laines wondered how long Marilyn would think about it. But it was likely too late. His death was probably very near. Sterling wouldn't interrupt an important meeting to take an impromptu rendezvous with Marilyn, even if he had ogled her, even drooled over her, in the past. The commander was much too meticulous in his planning. The idea was a last-ditch and ill-planned attempt at self-preservation—too little, too late.

Sterling swung his black leather chair around, regarding Laines with paper friendliness. "Come in and sit down."

Sterling sat behind his desk, back-dropped by intermittently beeping radar screens. Paper charts had also been pinned to the wall recently. They often huddled around what Sterling referred to as his "defense table" in another corner of the room. This was a different tact. Sterling wanted Laines square in his line of sight, not by his side.

On the defense table, which was more of an attack table really, a table representing Sterling's accoutrements of control, the red button, glass protective case flipped open, intermittently pulsated glowing red. It cast a faint pink hue on an otherwise sterile white fluorescently lit ceiling. The bomb that would destroy PEI was ready to launch.

Laines felt his palms become wet with sweat as he sat and faced Sterling. He hoped that the bothersome and recurring bead of sweat that often found the tip of his nose when he talked with Sterling would not reappear. *Show fear, show nervousness, and die.*

"Things went well," Laines said, clasping sweaty hands together. "I have Doctor Imes secured, and Velvet and Nathan are dead."

"That's good. Well done, Doctor Laines. Is Imes conscious?"

"Last I checked he was in a drug-induced coma, sir." *Buy some time, buy some time.* "I don't know what he took, but I can find out for you."

"I might want you to do that," Sterling said, running a hand over a clean-shaven face. He wore a general's military uniform decorated with many medals, some of which Laines suspected had been pinched from the late Commander Stiessman's luxurious quarters. His eyes were clear, alert, and bright. He looked fresh, alive, and well-rested. "But first, let's go over the results of your mission. Tell me how it went."

"Okay, sir." Before he began, Laines paused momentarily, wondering if he should tell Sterling about the HL Kane episode. But he realized in an instant that Sterling probably already knew. Not much got past the commander—may as well tell him. Laines began the account, starting with his decision to inject himself with HL Kane in an effort to insure the mission's success and help troops in trouble: "I'm so sorry for breaching protocol on that one. I just wanted to insure success, show you how competent I am, go the extra mile to protect you, sir. I assure you it will never happen again, no, no, never again. And I'm so sorry, but it got the results you wanted."

He told the commander how he located and invaded Imes's underground laboratory (at least with his giant hand), killing many Neanderthals and nasty giant flies in the process, and finally, just before leaving, killed Nathan and Velvet. He'd rescued Marilyn Buxton, the only soldier he found alive. He conveniently omitted that P-744-induced warriors no longer responded to the anti-violence code, and that their rage had reached the point of no return.

And no control. *No, the commander wouldn't like to hear that.*

As Laines talked, Sterling glanced occasionally at radar screens and every so often at the nuke aimed at PEI. He seemed anxious to get to it.

Laines finished the story. A silence ensued.

Commander Sterling stood up and started slowly pacing the room in front of his desk. Every so often he would walk behind Laines and Laines would quiver and shake, expecting a knife in the back at any second. The commander was on one of these rotations now, directly behind Laines. He bent down and breathed hot minty breath onto Laines's neck. "How did you kill Velvet and Nathan?"

Laines swung around to answer, jerking the chair and simultaneously fighting for control of his emotions. And his fear. But it was a losing battle to keep composure when faced with a man—no, an evil demon—such as this. The recurring bead of sweat had once more snaked its way to the tip of Laines's nose. It dangled and glittered like an unsculptured diamond under the harsh fluorescents. Laines faced Sterling, holding up a thumb. "I squashed them, sir. Right under this here thumb."

Sterling's eyes narrowed. He slapped the wooden desk hard with an open palm, didn't flinch from the pain it must have caused. "No you didn't, and you damn well know it."

Laines trembled, wiping the bead of sweat from his nose. He knew another one would be trailing it soon. "I don't know what you're talking about, sir." *A dumb thing to say. You're digging your grave.*

"Enough," Sterling said, the signature fly-swatting wave punctuating the word. "Don't play me for a fool, Laines. I credited you with more intelligence than that. I guess I was wrong."

"I'm so—"

"It's too late for that," Sterling interrupted, looking directly into Laines's magnified eyes. He returned to his desk and sat facing Laines. "Let me tell you something about control. Something my father, God rest his soul, taught me. Something my mother got very wrong. You see, she thought control was an illusion." Sterling's eyes glistened with psychosis, a mad scientist revealing a life-altering secret formula. He extended both arms to the ceiling. "But this is no illusion. I'm very close to a plan that will put me in bed with the North Koreans and give me complete control over the rest of the world. Oh, the politicians, my superiors, don't realize it yet, and when they do it'll be too late, but I'm on the cusp of the absolute pinnacle of my success as a man."

Laines was about to speak, but Sterling silenced him with the fly-swatting wave, this one inches from his perspiring nose. "You'll get your chance. It's my turn now. And I'm going to teach you a lesson. You see, my father taught me that in order to have control, to command respect, you can't tolerate insubordination. To do so would show weakness, weakness that would lead to mutiny, disrespect, and eventually a total disintegration of that control." Sterling was ranting now, obsessed with his monologue, regardless of whether Laines actually gave a fuck. "If I've failed anywhere in my rise to the top, it's not discovering the insubordination early enough. Bryce taught me to recognize weakness in its early stages and nip it in the bud. But in your case, I gave you the benefit of the doubt, one time too many, obviously. I overlooked a few things, figuring you'd come around to my way of thinking, come around and show me respect and subordination, two things fundamental to the control I so rightly deserve."

Beads of sweat snaked down Laines's forehead, onto his nose. He let them drip unchecked onto his white lab coat, for the moment mesmerized by the theatre of madness playing on the stage before him. He tried to think of a way out of this insane play. But all that came to him was a line from Shakespeare:

All the world's a stage,
And all the men and women merely players;
They have their exits and their entrances,

And man, do I need an exit right now. Think, fool. Think.

Sterling, now punctuating every sentence with animated gestures, continued: "But you didn't, did you? No ... in your silly little scientific mind, you made the unwise decision to grab some of that control, try and remove a steel building block from my mighty fortress of control. But in doing so, you erred. You should have realized my fortress of power and control is made of impenetrable steel ... impenetrable to fools like you ..."

Sterling opened a desk drawer, extracted a handgun, and placed it on the desk. After a moment, he regained control of his emotions and his expression grew calm, though his eyes flashed wildly with insanity. "Here's the thing," he said, picking up the handgun and massaging its barrel gently. "You're a baseball fan, right?"

Laines, now frozen in fear, nodded dumbly.

"Good, then you'll appreciate what I'm about to say. First you try and take some of my control. Strike one." He clicked the safety off and admired the weapon. "Then you show me a lack of respect. Strike two." He cocked the hammer, leveling it at Laines's head. "Then you demonstrate insubordination. Strike three, you're out."

Sterling fired.

Laines had already slid off the chair by the time the bullet whizzed past his head and tore into a thick wooden bull's-eye of sorts the commander had fastened to the wall directly behind his line of fire. Target practice.

Rolling, Laines glanced at the bull's-eye. *Motherfucker thought of everything.*

But Sterling was already upon him, firing the handgun at the rolling body. Bullets ricocheted off the polished steel floor, zinging every which way.

Laines winced as he felt one tear into his back. His backbone was on fire with hot pain. Laines was sure the bullet had shattered a vertebrae and the result would render him paraplegic or worse, quadriplegic. As he crawled, another shot grazed his ear, deafening. His ear buzzed wildly, but he continued crawling for his life, knowing with dread certainty he was actually crawling to his death.

The firing stopped and more pain seared through his chest as he felt a steel-toed, polished army boot connect, snapping ribs like candy canes and knocking him onto his back.

Sterling knelt down, lowering the business end of the handgun. His face, those evil glowing eyes and minty-fresh hot breath, came closer. He moved the barrel to Lainess's forehead and pressed it into hot, sweating skin. "I gave you a chance for much greater rewards," Sterling said. "And you went and fucked it all up."

His vision blurring from the pain, from the sweat dribbling into his eyes, Laines grunted, raised a fist and punched at the gun.

It connected and the weapon shook, discharging with a loud bang into Laines's neck. He felt hot blood bubbling forth like an angry geyser, soaking his chest, arms and neck.

Vision faded. *Now or never.* As Sterling raised the weapon, this time holding it firmly with two hands, and brought it toward Laines's head once more, Laines reached into his lab coat pocket, grabbed the syringe containing a triple dose of HL Kane, and plunged the needle deep into Sterling's neck.

Sterling's eyes widened in horror as he realized he had lost control of the situation. He removed a hand from the weapon and extracted the syringe from his neck. But it was too late. Laines had emptied its contents.

"Should have listened to your mother," Laines said. "Control's a fucking illusion."

Sterling tossed the syringe away angrily and gripped the weapon tightly with two hands.

But he had already started to grow. Like a not-so-jolly Green Giant, his face turning green with envy—or jealousy, or madness, or something—he sprouted to the ceiling. The handgun, now reduced to miniature size in comparison to his gigantic body, squirted loose and clanged to the floor. Like an Incredible Hulk transformation, his tiny but meticulously kept medal-clad uniform tore and stretched, finally falling to the floor, reduced to a mass of tethered fabric and tiny medals.

Then his enormous head slammed into the ceiling, shattering fluorescent lights. His body ballooned, filling up the room with its mass.

Laines watched, satisfied with the results of his brainchild. Maybe it was a success after all.

The ceiling impact knocked Sterling unconscious. Like a beached whale, his enormous frame crumpled over almost into a fetal position and grew silent.

Through blurred vision, Laines checked his watch. 6:33 pm. He crawled toward the red button, hoping to deactivate it. He had done enough stupid things in his life, and before he died, he wanted to at least die with the knowledge that, in the end, he had done the right thing. If there was a heaven, he wanted to meet Marilyn when her number for admission to the pearly gates was called.

He crawled.

The red light twinkled.

He reached the defense table, looking up in despair at its four-foot height. He no longer felt his legs and knew they had been clumping behind him in an uncooperative mass. He was a paraplegic.

With a blood-soaked hand, he reached for a table leg, anything he could use to pull himself up. The hand slipped from the steel table leg and he slid down to the floor.

The room grew black.

He could hear the heavy footfalls of soldiers thumping down the outside corridor, growing nearer.

He craned his neck, looking up in despair at the blinking red button. He took a deep breath and grabbed for the table leg once more. His grip caught, but started sliding.

Too much blood. So much blood. He didn't think he would make it.

Chapter Twenty-One

Nathan didn't want to think about it. He knew if he thought too much, maybe those familiar fear demons would creep back into his psyche and start singing that discordant chorus of discontent, the one he had heard so often in the past. It had haunted him really, and had the power to plant seeds of doubt about the whole plan, the whole disastrous world, the whole fucking futile purpose of his entire existence. But that was just negative thinking, he told himself, a defeatist attitude, glass-half-empty bullshit. Nothing more. Forget it. Get this done. Get this over with. Get off this fucking Island once and for all, leave all this shit behind and go ... where?

Neither of them knew. Leaving the small cabin in the woods, leaving their visions—is that what they were, visions?—behind, they had discussed it on route to Murray River. Get a boat, leave the Island, and cruise to ... wherever.

Velvet had been a little more proactive, but Nathan had been unwilling to acquiesce to her plan. She wanted to chart the boat to the aircraft carrier and put an end to Sterling's megalomaniac style of authority forever. But Nathan had convinced her they wouldn't stand a chance; as it was, they only had a snowball's chance in hell of even getting off the Island alive. Sterling would have choppers and planes patrolling the waters. He would spot them like a black fly on a whitewashed wall and squash them in an instant (not to mention giant black flies that could, in an instant, swarm in and attack en masse). It would be a little more than his dismissive fly-swatting gesture. It would represent a permanent end to their struggling existence.

So Velvet had agreed, at least conditionally. "Once we get on the boat, let's see how we feel," she said. "We're still going through changes. By then, maybe you'll want that nutcase dead too."

That seemed reasonable to Nathan. Once they got on the boat—if they managed to steal a boat—it would be much easier to convince Velvet of the danger lurking ahead, and perhaps above and beyond. He also knew that, once Sterling leveled PEI, the aircraft carrier would be long gone. They'd have no idea of its location. It would be an easy argument to win. Logic prevails. Prevailing logic.

So they had proceeded to Murray River, where they sat in the pick-up now, behind a ruined Esso service station, watching Neanderthals at the wharf loading supplies into boats.

The Neanderthals evidently had their own intelligence. The opportunistic savages knew the Island was about to become a fragmented archipelago drifting aimlessly through a contaminated Atlantic Ocean.

Outside, it was calm but cold. At least the flies and spiders were dormant at night. Military choppers, invading planes, and troops were long gone. Or long dead. The sky was hazy black-crimson, but a crescent moon peaked out through the post-apocalyptic curtain and provided a diffused gray light, their only light. By the light of the moon, they would make their attack.

They had entered in a roundabout fashion, taking back roads and pothole-filled side streets with decaying homes. Dead and decaying bodies slumped over porch railings or were splayed out on formerly well-manicured lush green lawns. Nathan had to swerve to avoid an elderly man lying in the middle of the road, chest riddled with bullets, twitching spasmodically, rasping, gurgling breath, blood foaming from his mouth. As Nathan slowed and peered out the window, the man said his own eulogy—"God help me ... God help us all"—breathed his last blood-bubbling breath, stiffened and died.

They had been sitting in silence for about five minutes, eyes adjusting to the light, surveying the scene—both mentally preparing for their fate, or their destiny, but either way, the point of no return.

Nathan looked at the clock. 6:33 pm. "It's time."

Velvet watched his eyes and pointed to a converted fishing boat. Its name was *Red River Blues*, perhaps suggesting and immortalizing in some weird way the carnage about to unfold. Swaying gently in the calm waters of Murray River (a salt-water river local fishermen once fished and used as a gateway to the Atlantic Ocean), its diesel engine chugged evenly. It sat to the left, away from most of The Neanderthals. It seemed the logical choice, as it offered some distance from the thirty or so Neanderthals. Two Neanderthals aboard *Red River Blues* fastened down supplies, while one stood at the wheel, ready to depart. They could hear faint conversations, and someone in authority barking out commands over the din of conversation.

Two boats departed, chugging out to the ocean and to an uncertain future.

"I'll go first," Velvet said evenly, pointing first to the largest population of scheming savages, then to *Red River Blues*. "I'm going to grenade those fuckers while you take out those bastards."

"Okay. I'll give you some cover fire."

Velvet nodded and prepared to open the door. Then she stopped momentarily, and looked at Nathan.

The driver door half open, he met her riveting gaze and stopped moving.

"If we don't make it," she said. "It's been a pleasure knowing you." She held out a hand.

He took it and shook it. "What, no kiss?"

"I'll think about it," she said, "Prove you're worthy."

They hit the ground running. Velvet, in the lead, unpinned first one, then two grenades and launched them a second apart at the Neanderthals.

Nathan opened fire.

One grenade exploded, sending screaming, shouting, dying Neanderthals airborne, their flaming bodies flying up and landing with a satisfying sizzle in the murky Murray River. The second grenade landed on the deck of a boat containing about six Neanderthals. A loud explosion shattered the vessel, sending debris mixed with dismembered body parts flying, some plunking into the water and being feasted upon by opportunistic hungry seagulls.

The pandemonium of a firefight erupted. Nathan provided cover fire as Velvet charged the remaining, stunned Neanderthals, weaving her machine gun methodically to and fro, spraying bullets.

Nathan sprinted toward *Red River Blues*, their escape boat, and one that was truly living up to its namesake. He stopped, crouched behind a wall of crates, and shot the man at the wheel in the chest three times. The remaining two ducked, returning fire. A tune by the Talking Heads played through his mind as he charged to the dock and leaped onto the deck off the boat. *We're on a road to nowhere ...*

A Neanderthal emerged and leveled a machine gun. A deafening spray of bullets rang out.

Nathan dove to the deck, shooting the Neanderthal in the head as he landed. The savage cried "Help me," then plunged into the water, a human feast for the frenzied, feeding, squawking seagulls, who had evidently decided it was much easier to attack the dead and dying than the live, battling humans. The path of least resistance. They had chosen wisely.

Nathan rolled around, frantically searching for the other Neanderthal. Where was Velvet?

The tune played on:

> *We're on a road to nowhere*
> *Come on inside*
> *Takin' that ride to nowhere*
> *We'll take that ride ...*

Nathan heard a snap, followed by a rush of searing pain to his chest, and knew instantly what it meant. One, maybe two ribs were broken or cracked. Either way, it would be a long time on the mend. He grimaced in pain, grabbed his chest, and rolled. Through blurred vision caused by blinding pain, he recognized the grinning, grizzled face looking down upon him.

It was the face of Mason Mulligan, black with hollow sockets where eyes glowed red in the suffused gray light. It was the face of the grim reaper.

And it was the face of the Devil himself.

"Whaa ...," Nathan said between panting, raspy breaths. The kick to the ribs had also winded him. "I thought you were dead?"

"No," Mason said. "That giant fuck, whoever he was, left me for dead. But in the end, it was his girlfriend who saved my life. She was in trouble, so he pitched me in a pile of rubble. I was lucky enough to land on a pile of decomposing bodies. A soft pile, I might add."

Mason unsheathed a large sword. "But you'll be very dead, very soon." He raised the sword. "The old-fashioned way. You know there's no shame in dying by the sword. Defeated warriors used to throw themselves upon it as a final act of sacrifice. Throw themselves upon it rather than let the enemy capture or kill them."

With both hands he arched the sword high in the air. It glinted in the light of the crescent moon. "So don't be ashamed. I'd let you do it, but I know you don't have the stones for that, do you? But not to worry, I'll relieve you of the responsibility and gladly take over where your manhood fails."

"Fuck you," Nathan said. In spite of the pain, a surge of adrenaline was rapidly clearing his vision and parking the discomfort in some unoccupied parking stall of his mind. "You won't get off here alive. We're all going to die."

The sword was getting closer. Nathan knew at any second it would come at full thrust, plunging into his heart.

But the sound of a voice stopped the blade. It was Joey Zidewick, Mason's whipping boy, alongside another Neanderthal. They held a bleeding Velvet Jones. They'd probably brought her to witness Nathan's execution before they executed her. "We've got her, boss," Joey said.

"Bring her here," Mason said, delivering a kick to Nathan's head just because he could. And because he felt like it. "I think this is something she needs to see."

They escorted Velvet to the edge of the dock and stopped. She struggled futilely. One of the men holding her was the size of a linebacker, with arms bigger than Nathan's thighs.

"Velvet Jones," Mason said. "We meet again."

"You're a fucking pig," she said and spit blood on the dock, along with a molar that had been punched loose.

"I resent that," Mason said. "In fact, when I raped your daughter Lisa, I made it a point to be very gentle with her. I don't know if she appreciated the baseball bat to the head afterwards, perhaps she didn't think that was too gentle. But I guarantee you she enjoyed the sex. I'm a regular Don Juan with women. Didn't you know? Oh, but I'll show you, Velvet ..." He raised the sword again.

"You disgust me," Velvet said, struggling fiercely now. "I'm going to kill you ... you fucking sicko."

"Haven't you learned any manners? Don't interrupt a man while he's talking. What was I saying ... oh yeah ... I'll show you what really good sex is like once I end the life of your stoneless, sissy boyfriend over here ..."

"Fuck off, you fucking freak of nature," Nathan said.

"I'll let that one slide," Mason said, grinning wickedly. "Joey, this here is an example of a man with no stones." Mason pointed to the sword. "And this here is what he's going to get. Let that be a lesson to you, boy ... how many times do I have to tell you? ... grow some fucking stones."

"Okay," Joey said calmly, releasing Velvet, drawing his gun, and firing two shots. They tore through each red, twinkling evil eye of his former boss. "I think that's a good idea."

Mason Mulligan dropped the sword and Nathan rolled as the glinting blade plummeted toward his head. Mason crashed to the deck of the boat, mouth agape in an agonizing look of fear and shock. In death, as in life, he looked crazy.

Joey pointed the gun at the ape holding Velvet. "You got any bright ideas, fat boy? Let her go."

The ape released Velvet, who jumped on the boat and began tearing at a very dead Mason Mulligan's bloody eye sockets.

"Every man for himself," the ape said, turning and running toward a disembarking boat of Neanderthals, who, maybe because their boss was dead, or maybe because the self-preservation need overrode any murderous designs, had stopped firing and were leaving, chugging out to sea on their respective vessels.

Joey, meanwhile, calmly untied the ropes of *Red River Blues*, tossed them aboard, and stood watching in some far-away crazed amusement as Velvet, now screaming hysterically, tore large chunks of flesh from Mason's bloodied face.

It took a few minutes for Nathan to calm her. But he finally did, and they pitched Mason's fat dead ass overboard so he could have a proper burial at sea.

Joey watched in strange amusement as Velvet grabbed the helm and started to maneuver the boat away from shore.

Nathan turned to Joey. "Thank you."

"Don't mention it," he said. "Joey Zidewick's the name. It was a pleasure. Trust me. Bon voyage."

In Nathan's mind, the Talking Heads tune—briefly interrupted—resumed:

> *We're on a road to nowhere*
> *We're on a road to nowhere*
> *We're on a road to nowhere*
>
> *There's a city in my mind*
> *Come along and take that ride*
> *And it's all right, baby it's all right.*

"Aren't you coming with us, Joey?" Nathan asked.

Joey offered a toothy grin and put the gun to his temple. "It's all right. I've finally grown some stones. My work is done here."

He pulled the trigger and blew his brains out.

Chapter Twenty-Two

Nathan, who thought he had the stomach for plenty of gore, promptly put his aching head over the side of the boat after Joey Zidewick blew his brains out and vomited. Maybe it was the kick to the ribs and the boot to the brain that contributed to the nausea. He didn't know, but he puked a long, slimy, yellow stream into the water as blood-soaked and silent Velvet Jones glided *Red River Blues* out into the ocean.

The other Neanderthals had a headstart, and there was no point following. Velvet found their own course, putting some distance between them and the savages. After a while, they were alone with their thoughts in rising ocean swells, waiting for the end of the Island and maybe the end of the world.

The encounter with Mason had taken the fight out of them for now, Nathan thought, sitting on a plastic chair bolted to the deck and wiping away yellow strands of puke from his chin and neck. A fresh bolt of pain shot up from the offending ribs and he grimaced, rubbing the injury. It only seemed to make things worse so he withdrew his hand and thought about The Neanderthals. They had been quick to cow-tow to the meanest son of a bitch in the valley, but maybe that's just how it was when structure and authority were absent. People gravitate to law and order, any law and order, as long as it keeps them alive a little longer. Mason had come along at an opportune time and showed the people a maligned direction. They had followed and appointed him their leader. Who else did they have to turn to? They had to form some kind of tribe—power in numbers, to keep them away from predators, including an evil government. What did George Orwell say in his allegory, *Animal Farm*? *Absolute power corrupts absolutely.* The existing government, the military, and Commander Rice Sterling were living proof of that.

But maybe, just maybe, now that these Neanderthals were free of their ruthless leader, there was some hope of reformation. Maybe these escapees, if they lived, would turn a corner, begin a life with at least a shred of humanity. Joey proved that was possible. At least that was the hope Nathan clung to. Otherwise, he thought, humanity was doomed.

And what about Velvet? He had no idea how the news that Mason had raped and murdered her daughter would affect her in the long run, if there was a long run. But wasn't Lisa happy now, in the Second Realm with Cadence, who had also been raped and murdered by Neanderthals? Cadence, with her loving heart, was just the person to mend the assaulted soul of the young girl, and show her the positives in life, that glass-half-full attitude Cadence was known and admired by her peers for.

It had been fifteen minutes since they had left the Murray River wharf, and Nathan hadn't uttered a word to Velvet, knowing she needed time to process the recent tragic news about Lisa. Maybe in time the wound would scab over and heal up, perhaps producing a small scar—she could certainly never forget something like that—but a scar that would not taint her version of humankind even more that it already was. A scar that perhaps would not haunt her for the rest of her life, but would heal and become something she might one day be able to live with.

"Speaking of life," Nathan said aloud, without even realizing he had said it, "how much time do we have?"

He went and stood beside Velvet. She was looking out to sea and steering somberly. A painted green wooden plaque fastened to the dashboard proclaimed: *There are only two rules on this boat. 1. Don't question authority. 2. If you have a question, refer to rule 1.*

He didn't know if she had heard him. "Velvet, do you know what time it is?"

She pointed to what initially Nathan thought was the plaque, but then he realized it was a digital bedside clock that the previous owner had obviously modified and installed into the boat's dashboard, right beside the plaque. It read 6:57 pm.

"Shit, we don't have much time. Do you think we're out of the blast zone?"

She looked at him, defeated. "I don't care anymore, Nathan." Her voice was tinged with emotion. "Can't you see? Open your eyes. Everything's fucked up. This struggle is fucked up, you're fucked up. I'm fucked up. The whole world is fucked up beyond repair, the whole fucking wor—"

Refer to rule number one, Nathan thought grimly. But that's all he would think.

A thunderous boom shook the small vessel. They spun around and watched the mushroom-shaped fiery red explosion, trailed by thick black smoke, rising from what was once Prince Edward Island, "The Gentle Island," as tourist brochures and maps once proudly proclaimed. Then the crimson aftershock fanned out, the booming sound became deafening, and a wall of death raced toward them at blinding speed.

Nathan's ears buzzed like a million angry suicidal flies bouncing off a wall.

The tiny vessel was thrust up a massive, rapidly growing wave. Nathan grabbed Velvet and clung to her as the powerful force tossed them through the air like Raggedy Anne and Raggedy Andy.

The blinding light and heat stung his eyes, stung his body like a million tiny, swiftly penetrating swords. He knew he was dying. The whole world was dying. Velvet was right. Refer to rule number one. The whole world's fucked up beyond repair.

Then consciousness disappeared.

And an all-consuming black void appeared.

Chapter Twenty-Three

The hot sun reappeared as a puffy white cloud drifted lazily past, back-dropped by bright blue sky. It was mid-afternoon, a picture-perfect day on the Atlantic Ocean. The warm ocean waters were calm, the luxurious yacht on which he relaxed was perfectly comfortable, and the company was good, if not goddess-like. Yes, goddess-like was more like it, Doctor Stanley Imes decided as he book-marked his place in George Orwell's allegoric fable *Animal Farm* and placed the book on a steel end table. He stretched, savoring the warmth of the sun's healthful rays, and decided it was time for a drink.

In the past, he hadn't been much of a drinker, a teetotaler really. But, hell, he was in the Caribbean, only a mile or so from Ocean World Marina, just outside the small but lively beach community of Costamber, Puerto Plata, in the Dominican Republic. In keeping with the culture and customs, perhaps an afternoon rum and Coke was in order before dinner.

He rose from the foam-padded bed-style lawn chair, yawned, scratched his mop of curly hair, and headed below deck.

Clad in a skimpy pink bikini, its connecting strands almost as thin as dental floss, her voluptuously overflowing, ample endowments left little to the imagination. But Imes was still able to imagine a multitude of sexual delights that lay ahead.

Busy making a fruit salad and preparing drinks in the modern, fully-equipped bar, Marilyn Buxton spun around, smiled teasingly, and approached Imes. She was truly any man's dream girl come true, Imes thought. She handed him a drink in a tall glass with lots of crushed ice; just how he liked it.

"Here you go," she said, pecking him on the mouth. "Your afternoon drink."

Imes smiled as she returned to the bar to fix her drink. "Hey, you read my mind."

"I'm more than just a pretty face," she said with a wink, flashing that winning smile.

And indeed she had proven she was much more than a pretty face. Even though Imes still trifled with the notion that Marilyn might be little more than an opportunistic goddess who was cunningly adept at using her prodigious gifts and talents to get her way, one part of him asserted that it didn't really matter anymore. He was going to die one day. We all were. At least he wouldn't die alone and unhappy. Even if she had her own agenda, Marilyn had showed him love and tenderness the likes of which he had never experienced before.

And she had gone one giant leap forward. She had saved his life, rescued him from the clutches of madman Commander Rice Sterling. She had helped him to rally troops, who were quick to insubordinate once they realized their leader was lying unconscious; the bitter irony of it all, trapped in his control room, his command central.

By the time Imes reached the control room, defecting troops at his side, Doctor Jeffery Laines was already dead. In his last minutes he had scrambled up to the defense table, a trail of blood marking his progress. They found him slouched over, an outstretched hand an inch short of the keypad that would deactivate the bomb targeted for PEI. In his dying moments, he had tried but ultimately failed to do the right thing, at least when it came to saving the Island. The nuke had obliterated, at least the western portion of it.

But Laines had immobilized the madman, and had bought Imes time, time to inform Prime Minister Eliot Masterson that Sterling, in conjunction with North Korea, had been hatching a plan for absolute control. A plan so wicked and devious it also included the president's death. It had only taken a short conversation for Masterson to give the order to abandon ship. "Blow it to shit, along with that scumbag, and then take a well-deserved break in the Caribbean while we pick up the pieces and try and figure out what to do next."

The Caribbean, Imes thought, climbing the steps into bright warm sunshine. As if the invisible hand of God had wrapped a protective layer around it, the Dominican Republic had been spared the worldwide devastation.

Imes paused at the doorway, glancing down at Marilyn, who had bent over, displaying barely-contained curvaceous buttocks. She was returning a bottle of Coke to the fridge. "You coming up, honey?"

She closed the fridge and turned around, that seductive smile reappearing instantly. "I'll be up in a minute, babe. I think it's time to wake the lovebirds."

"Good idea," Imes said. "Not good for them to sleep too long. Not in their condition."

Epilogue

Waking up slowly, seeing the bright smile, feeling the warmth of Marilyn's hand on his shoulder, Nathan's knee-jerk reaction was to freeze, but only for a split-second before he took a few deep breaths and realized it was all part of what Imes called his condition—post-traumatic stress disorder, among other things.

He felt his muscles slowly relax.

Beside him, Velvet bolted upright at the intrusion, snatched a handgun from under her pillow, and leveled it at Marilyn's head momentarily before she too realized it was also part of her condition, the PTSD, among other things.

Velvet took a few deep breaths, un-cocked, and placed the gun on a bedside table. Hardened, battle-ready features softened and she looked embarrassedly from Marilyn to gun, gun to Marilyn.

Marilyn, who had jumped back in shock, regained her soft and playful demeanor. "I'm sorry. I should have knocked. I should have known better. Especially in your condition. I won't do it again. I'll knock. I promise." She went to the door. Turning around, she said, "Just wanted to let you know there's breakfast ready for you. And we're having drinks on deck if you want to join us."

"Thanks," Nathan said. "We'll be out in a minute."

She closed the door and left.

Velvet kissed Nathan and walked into the bathroom, carrying the handgun. His eyes followed her athletic body, clad in black lace bra and panties.

His thoughts drifted back to his condition—their condition.

The blast that destroyed most of the Island had knocked them through a doorway leading to the bilge and bathroom of the boat, offering some protection from the giant waves. There, severely concussed, they had drifted helplessly for forty-eight hours before Imes, flying co-pilot in a rescue military chopper, had plucked them out of a ferocious storm and rescued them from certain death. He had received permission from the president to have them accompany him on aforementioned vacation; after all, Imes still had to monitor their condition to insure the P-744 antidote was doing what it was designed for, ridding them of the disastrous P-744 effects.

Inside the bathroom, Nathan began brushing his teeth as Velvet slipped into the shower. What of the P-744 effects? Was he normal? He and Velvet had been on the infirmary-equipped super yacht a month now, recovering from the ordeal. Velvet's injuries had proven to be non-life threatening and, at least physically, she was on the mend.

Nathan's ribs still pained him. He had to sleep on his right side now. Sleeping on his left, the ribs ached too much and he inevitably had to change positions. He'd probably have to for life.

Of course, that was the physical part.

There was always the mental.

At times he found it difficult to process information, probably a result of too many concussive blows to the head, particularly the big blast from the nuke and the amnesia-producing concussive fall before any of this mess had even started. Mid-conversation, he would gap out and lose his train of thought. He noticed Velvet doing the same thing occasionally. According to Imes, only time would tell how fully they might recover from the concussions. ("The brain has an amazing capacity to regenerate or retrain itself to use other areas, but we'll just have to see.") But, thinking about it now, he realized the gaps were becoming fewer and farther between. At least, that was what he wanted to believe.

There were other nagging questions. Did the antidote work? Nathan smiled. He hadn't felt the violent rage of the past in over a month. It was like a giant anchor of dread—and yes, psychosis—had been lifted from his chest.

They never spoke of Cadence or Lisa again, perhaps both unwilling to remove the scabs from old wounds improperly healed. Maybe in time they *would* be able to discuss their loved ones, but not yet, not now.

This time was their time to heal. Someone, and Nathan had no idea who, once said, "You have to look after yourself before you look after others." And that's what they were doing. Their mutual attraction had grown, developing naturally into true love. Even Imes, last night over drinks and dinner on the boat, had proudly proclaimed, "I think the antidote works. And I was wrong. You guys fell in love naturally."

Nathan knew both of them still had their issues—hell, no one's perfect, right? And he knew they had a long way to go in an uncertain future. But he had something more valuable than anything money could buy. He had true love, a powerful connection that had overcome many seemingly insurmountable obstacles. That thought suddenly brought a giddy excitement to his usual slow-to-wake-up morning demeanor.

In the shower, Velvet began singing a song by The Beatles. She sang low, the words barely audible at first, but then her melodious voice developed power and conviction:

"There's nothing you can make that can't me made
No one you can save that can't be saved
Nothing you can do but you can learn how to be you in time
It's easy

All you need is love
All you need is love
All you need is love, love
Love is all you need ..."

Listening to the last lyric, sung so melodically and with so much joy, Nathan peeled back the curtain. Velvet, nude, beautiful, hot water cascading off perky breasts, curled her finger toward him. "Get in. Now."

"With pleasure." Nathan climbed in and kissed her ravenously. He pulled away, staring directly into her beautiful green eyes. "I love you."

She arched a black eyebrow in mock interrogation. "Not genetic modification?"

"No," he said, beginning to explore the erogenous zones of her body. "I really love you, Velvet. I love you so much that even if I just had a fragment of you it would be enough. But I have you, all of you, don't I?"

She put her hands on his shoulders and pushed him back a little as the hot water cascaded off their heads. "Are you sure?" she asked.

"I've never been more sure of anything in my life."

"Good," she said. "Then I love you too."

******

About two hours later, after they had breakfasted on fruit salad, scrambled eggs, toast and fresh, non-radiation-contaminated orange juice, they reclined in luxurious lawn chairs on the deck of the luxurious yacht, soaking up the sun's wonderfully life-giving warm rays, drinking, smoking, and talking.

Imes was nestled in close with Marilyn, one hand occasionally strolling down to her stomach while he spoke. He had a pretty good alcohol buzz going.

Hell, so did Nathan and Velvet, for that matter. Reclining next to Velvet, Nathan held her hand as they listened to Imes.

"I have important news," Imes said, ringing his half-full glass with a tea spoon.

Imes put the glass on the table, pecked a smiling Marilyn on the cheek, and spoke: "I had a conversation with the prime minister today."

"You did?" Velvet asked, butting her cigarette, taking a swallow of her drink, and squeezing Nathan's hand. "And what did his highness have to say for himself?"

Imes paused, cleared his throat, and removed his wandering hand from Marilyn's navel, not that she appeared to be minding it there. "He apologized for any discomfort the government-sanctioned experiments might have caused, thanked you profusely for your bravery and loyalty, and promised that from now on, you will be well taken care of.

He even said he's making inroads with the North Koreans to restore order and repopulate what's left of the world."

"And you believed him?" Velvet asked. "After everything that's happened?"

After a moment, Imes said, "Yes, I think I do." Then, looking at his half-full glass, he added, "I prefer to look at the glass as half full."

"Cheers to that," Marilyn said. They clinked glasses and drank.

Imes continued; he talked about how the effects of HL Kane were fortunately short-lived and the giant insects were dying off, as well as the zombies. The Neanderthals, those still alive and with any fight left in them, were being destroyed by elite military forces. And the Canadian government was reconstructing huge sections of land in British Columbia that would soon be fit for human habitation.

Imes even admitted P-744, his brainchild, was a huge mistake and a monumental disaster. It had been permanently shelved. On and on he went about a future that was getting brighter by the day. Future's-so-bright-I-gotta-wear-shades kind of future, the kind everyone would embrace.

Velvet rebuked many of Imes's claims, at times even interrupting him to play devil's advocate.

As his mind drifted, Nathan snatched at and recorded many of Velvet's comments:

"I wouldn't trust them. Any government that would fuck with our heads once will surely do it again."

"Reconstructing? What, now the government has to reconstruct land they destroyed?"

"*P-744 shelved? I'll believe that when I see it. It's too valuable to the nutcases in power to ever shelve it. Either they're shooting you a line of shit, or you're shooting us a line of shit. Or both.*"

"*You're right, Imes. The future's so bright I gotta wear shades.*"

And the kicker: "*You've heard it before ... absolute power corrupts absolutely.*"

While picking up these snippets of dialogue, Nathan's mind continued to drift deeper to that one question, the one that remained perched atop a steep cliff deep within the vast mountain range of his mind, dormant but ready to plunge into that bottomless black abyss of despair at any second. The question concerned the Second Realm. It needed to be asked. It needed to be answered. Did it exist, or was it the shell-shocked survivor of a war with insanity; a war he had almost lost?

He had learned Imes had experimented with a drug, perhaps a modified version of P-744, Imes thought would transport him to the Second Realm. The drug had evidently removed Mary Anne from this Earth and into the land of the dead, fulfilling Ed's desire to have one of the few women who had showed him true love by his side. Fulfilling, really, Nathan's promise to his friend.

But Nathan was still haunted by the nightmares. Nightmares that often woke him up in the middle of the night, sweat-soaked, panting for breath, frozen with fear. Horrible nightmares that all seemed to offer variations of the same theme. Ed in the Second Realm with his grandmother Mary Anne. The dream would often begin happily, like the one last night, for example. Ed was on a puffy cloud, sitting at the dinner table. Mary Anne put down a hearty bowl of stew for her grandson. Ed ate. They laughed and joked. But then, out of the corner of a grotesquely expanding blood-red eye, Ed spotted Nathan, grinned wickedly, and said: "One day you'll know, my friend. One day you'll know. And you'll realize the import of my words."

And always, while struggling to escape the nightmares, struggling to swim out of this terrifying state of unconsciousness, the words would flood forth, penetrate Nathan's mind like a stray bullet, and ricochet around his skull with stinging force, echoing the same chilling words: *You're going to die ... painfully ... very soon.*

"Do you feel all right?" Velvet asked. "You're white."

Nathan looked at her. Concern was etched in her brow, love in her eyes. He was about to dismiss the query and tell her he was just fine and everything was just great, thank you very much. But everything wasn't that great regarding the Second Realm or his nightmares. And he wasn't totally fine, thank you very much for asking. His psyche was tormented. Since their rescue, he had never spoken of it to Velvet.

But now he had to get it off his chest.

For liquid courage, he drained half his drink. He would need another one soon.

He released Velvet's hand and addressed Doctor Imes, whose wandering hand had once more found Marilyn's bare mid-section. "What about the Second Realm?"

"What about it?"

"Does it exist? Did you go there?"

Like her flat stomach was a red-hot stovetop burner, the doctor's hand jerked away from Marilyn's navel. Imes's features darkened. He removed his glasses. "There's something I never told you about P-744."

Drinks lowered onto tables. Cigarette butts squashed into ashtrays. He had their undivided attention.

Imes continued: "One of the side effects of P-744 was this Second Realm concept. Other subjects had it. You felt it rather strongly. I didn't want to say anything about it earlier because I hadn't sorted it out. So I developed a modified version of P-744 that I thought would transport me to this other plane of existence. You remember how dire things got. Surely you could understand my reasons. But all it did was transport me into a psychological hell, a living, torturous hell almost akin to what you and Velvet just experienced in the real world. Myself too, I might add. But, in the end, the drug didn't take me to any other dimension, or to some form of heaven. All it did was catapult me to a state of near-total madness."

He took another large swallow of his drink. With an unsteady hand, he set the glass down. "And I'm glad it's over and Marilyn—I still don't know how she did it—managed to bring me out of that coma and rescue me from that hell." He kissed her on the cheek. "I've got news for you, Nathan. The Second Realm doesn't exist. Heaven doesn't exist. Devils, maybe, but certainly not angels." He kissed Marilyn again and the wandering hand crawled toward her navel. "Except this one right here. She's the only angel I know of. And she's real ... and right by my side." He turned to her. "Aren't you, sweetie?"

"Forever," she said, wrapping her arms around him.

Imes went on: "I know you're still having nightmares. It's a symptom of post-traumatic stress disorder. Trust me. With time and the right treatment, I'm sure they'll go away."

"Thank you very much all the same," Velvet said. She too had been having terrible nightmares. "And no disrespect or offense intended, but I don't think Nathan or I are waiting in line with baited breath for any more of your *treatment*. I'm sorry. We've sampled about enough of it for the time being. But thanks anyway."

Nathan wasn't surprised at the outburst, nor did he try and contain it. When Velvet wanted to vent, he let Velvet vent, unless he wanted to be on the receiving end of her wrath. Besides, he was in full agreement with her. Wasn't "thanks anyway" the equivalent of telling someone to fuck off?

Velvet stood up abruptly. "I'm tired." She looked at Nathan, arching an eyebrow. Come with me.

Velvet began leaving.

Nathan picked up their glasses and followed. "To be continued," he said, before disappearing into the lower quarters.

He could faintly hear Imes's voice trailing off as he refilled their glasses at the bar. "I know you guys don't forgive me yet, maybe you never will. But some day, I hope for your forgiveness and your understanding. I love you. I love you guys, I really do."

Imes loved everybody when he was drunk. Nathan had seen the display once before since arriving on the yacht. Maybe the former teetotaler was wracked by guilt and was becoming an alcoholic. If anyone had a good reason, it was certainly Imes.

******

A short time later, lying with Velvet and getting drunk—they were on vacation, after all—Nathan thought about Imes's revelation. It had whacked him in the head like a sledgehammer. After some discussion with Velvet, he realized she too had been punched hard in the solar plexus by the proclamation. While they didn't discuss the significance, they knew. Imes's news, if true, meant Cadence and Lisa were not happily and peacefully cavorting in some idyllic other dimension akin to heaven. Maybe they were suffering in some dark and dreary pit of horrors, for all they knew now.

Perhaps on some level they still despised Doctor Imes and his willingness to use human test subjects in the development of a super race of warriors. This distrust was warranted, Nathan supposed. Megalomaniacs always said their work was for the greater good of humanity, but typically it was for little more than self-aggrandizement.

Oh well. At least Imes had a conscience. He had saved their lives, hadn't he?

And they didn't have to believe him.

As if reading his mind—they had become intimately in tune with each other's emotions—Velvet set her drink down, crawled up on Nathan's bare chest, and looked into his eyes. "We don't have to believe him, you know. We don't have to believe what Imes said."

"I know. I don't believe him."

"I don't believe him either."

Velvet kissed Nathan. "God, sometimes I don't know what I'd do without you. At least we've got that."

"We do, baby. I love you more than words can express. I think I'd go completely nuts if it weren't for you."

She smothered him with kisses. "You probably already are."

"I know."

"Hell, I probably am too, for that matter."

"I know."

She slapped him playfully on the cheek. "You're not supposed to agree with *that*."

They stared up at the ceiling quietly for a few minutes, listening to the playful laughter of Imes and Marilyn on deck getting drunker and friskier. The alcohol was taking its toll on Nathan as well. He felt tired, a head buzzing with unanswered questions and pickled by too many drinks.

A tune, Eric Clapton's *Wonderful Tonight*, floated across his swimming mind. He supposed his life had come down to exhilarating moments of happiness juxtaposed with terrifying moments of fear. He had hoped he would find some straight and even stretches on a racetrack that seemed so full of death-defying hairpin corners. He now realized that in this crazy, mixed up, fucked up world, moments of true happiness were scarce and fleeting. But, in that instant, he vowed to cherish, savor, and at least try to remember them.

And, for the moment, Eric Clapton's lyrics calmed him; brought him a moment of simple joy and peace:

We go to a party and everyone turns to see
This beautiful lady that's walking around with me.
And then she asks me, "Do you feel all right?"
And I say, "Yes, I feel wonderful tonight."
I feel wonderful because I see
The love light in your eyes.
And the wonder of it all
Is that you just don't realize how much I love you.

An hour later, as the thick hand of sleep gently imposed its will, Nathan saw Ed's face again; it was a black, monstrous, grinning face with large red eye sockets shedding tears of blood.

Nathan's heart fluttered and skipped a beat. Sweat trickled down his forehead.

Then Ed spoke the words.

But they didn't have the same ring, the same horrible finality as before. "You're going to die. But, I was wrong. Not soon, Nathan. Not slowly and painfully, either. At peace, and not for a long time. And with the one you love. Don't listen to Imes. The Second Realm is real ... The Second Realm is beautiful. It's just me. I'm still a little cursed, still a little crazy ..."

Then the grotesque image of Edward Sole's assaulted soul vanished.

Nathan unknowingly removed his hands from his ears. A slight smile pursed his lips. Unconsciously wrapping his arms tightly around Velvet, he drifted deeper into a contented, dreamless, and restful sleep—the first in a very long time.

The End

Also by William Blackwell

Phantom Rage, Poison Rage, Infected Rage
Nightmare's Edge
Resurrection Point
Brainstorm
A Head for an Eye
Rule 14
Blood Curse
Black Dawn
Assaulted Souls
Assaulted Souls II
Assaulted Souls III
The Strap
The End is Nigh
Orgon Conclusion
Freaky Franky
The Witch's Tombstone
The Dark Menace
In Your Dreams
Macabre Alley
Tales of Damnation

The Strap Preview

"I loved this story, the plot was fast-paced but not too quick, the characters blend together really well especially Gray and Derrick. There's plenty of tension, suspense and action to keep you flying through the pages... I really enjoyed it and will be recommending it to my blogger friends." -Amazon

When Gray Eagleson remembers the strap, it brings back horrific images of pain, suffering and humiliation in the public school system.

Emotionally and financially strapped, he decides a trip to Ecuador is exactly what he needs for a fresh start. Before departing, he connects with Adriana Enrique on an internet dating site, promising to meet her on his arrival. He also helps his best friend Derrick Richmond evict some biker tenants involved in a marijuana grow-operation in one of Derrick's rental properties. One of the bikers, Stuart Treblecoch, aka The Strap, threatens to kill Gray for tossing biker belongings into a blazing backyard inferno.

Arriving in Ecuador, Gray soon discovers the idyllic vacation has turned into a life-and-death struggle. Adriana's erratic behavior casts a black shadow of doubt over his optimistic expectations, and he is terrified to learn The Strap is hunting him down. As the tension and violence ratchet up, Gray believes the mind-altering and spiritually enlightening drug ayahuasca is his only hope for salvation.

A taut psychological thriller, *The Strap* ushers you full-throttle deep inside the exotic sights and sounds of Ecuador while also exposing the very real dangers that exist.

Through Gray's harrowing journey for personal redemption and survival, we discover the frailties and insecurities of the human condition and the ever-present need for companionship at the heart of human nature.

About the Author

Canadian dark fiction author William Blackwell studied journalism at Mount Royal University and English literature at The University of British Columbia. He worked as a journalist and a newspaper editor for many years before pursuing his passion for storytelling. His novels have been characterized as graphic, edgy, and at times terrifying. Currently living on a secluded acreage on Prince Edward Island, Blackwell finds much of his inspiration from Mother Nature, odd people, traveling, and bizarre nightmares.

Author Comments

Thank you for reading this book. I would be eternally grateful if you would post a book review on your favorite book retailer website. A positive review is the highest compliment a writer can receive and also helps readers discover new books. Reviews are crucial to the success of any author. You don't have to say much. A few sentences will suffice.

In other news, I have a gift for you. Complete the signup form below with your name and email address and download a FREE copy of *Resurrection Point*, a dark tale about the horrifying consequences of experimenting with death and resurrection. You're only agreeing to be kept up to date on blog posts, new releases, and freebies. I promise I won't spam you and you can unsubscribe at any time.

Thanks again for your support.

http://www.wblackwell.com/free-ebook/